YORK NOTES

THE CRUCIBLE

ARTHUR MILLER

NOTES BY DAVID LANGSTON AND
MARTIN J. WALKER

Longman
is an imprint of

PEARSON

York Press

The right of David Langston and Martin J. Walker to be identified as Authors of
this Work has been asserted by them in accordance with the Copyright, Designs
and Patents Act 1988

YORK PRESS
322 Old Brompton Road, London SW5 9JH

PEARSON EDUCATION LIMITED
Edinburgh Gate, Harlow,
Essex CM20 2JE, United Kingdom
Associated companies, branches and representatives throughout the world

First published 1997
New edition 2002
This new and fully revised edition 2011

10 9 8 7 6 5 4 3

ISBN 978–1–4082–7004–2

Illustrated by Virginia Gray; and Neil Gower (p. 6)
Photograph of Arthur Miller reproduced by kind permission of Alamy Limited
Phototypeset by Border Consultants, Dorset
Printed in China (CTPS/03)

CONTENTS

PART FOUR
KEY CONTEXTS AND THEMES

PART FIVE
LANGUAGE AND STRUCTURE

PART SIX
GRADE BOOSTER

PART ONE: INTRODUCTION

Study and revision advice

There are two main stages to your reading and work on *The Crucible*. Firstly, the study of the play as you read it. Secondly, your preparation or revision for the exam or controlled assessment. These top tips will help you with both.

READING AND STUDYING THE PLAY – DEVELOP INDEPENDENCE!

- Try to engage and respond **personally** to the characters, ideas and story – not just for your enjoyment, but also because it helps you develop your own **independent ideas and thoughts** about *The Crucible*. This is something that examiners are very keen to see.

- **Talk** about the text with friends and family; ask questions in class; put forward your own viewpoint – and, if you have time, **read around** the text to find out about *The Crucible*.

- Take time to **consider** and **reflect** on the **key elements** of the play; keep your own notes, mind-maps, diagrams, scribbled jottings about the characters and how you respond to them; follow the action as it progresses (what do you think might happen?); discuss the main themes and ideas (what do *you* think it is about? Religious persecution? Love? Power and land?); pick out language that impresses you or makes an **impact**, and so on.

- Treat your studying **creatively**. When you write essays or give talks about the book make your responses creative. Think about using really clear ways of explaining yourself, use unusual **quotations**, well-chosen **vocabulary**, and try powerful, persuasive ways of beginning or ending what you say or write.

REVISION – DEVELOP ROUTINES AND PLANS!

- **Good revision** comes from **good planning**. Find out when your exam or controlled assessment is and then plan to look at key aspects of *The Crucible* on different days or times during your revision period. You could use these Notes – see **How can these Notes help me?** – and add dates or times when you are going to cover a particular topic.

- Use **different ways** of revising. Sometimes talking about the text and what you know/don't know with a friend or member of the family can help; other times, filling a sheet of A4 with all your ideas in different coloured pens about a character, for example Joe, can make ideas come alive; other times, making short lists of quotations to learn, or numbering events in the plot can assist you.

- **Practise plans** and **essays**. As you get nearer the 'day', start by looking at essay **questions** and writing short bulleted plans. Do several plans (you don't have to write the whole essay); then take those plans and add details to them (quotations, linked ideas). Finally, using the advice in **Part Six: Grade Booster**, write some practice essays and then check them out against the advice we have provided.

EXAMINER'S TIP

Prepare for the exam/assessment! Whatever you need to bring, make sure you have it with you – books, if you're allowed, pens, pencils – and that you turn up on time!

Introducing *The Crucible*

Setting

The Crucible is set in the New England town of Salem, Massachusetts, in 1692.

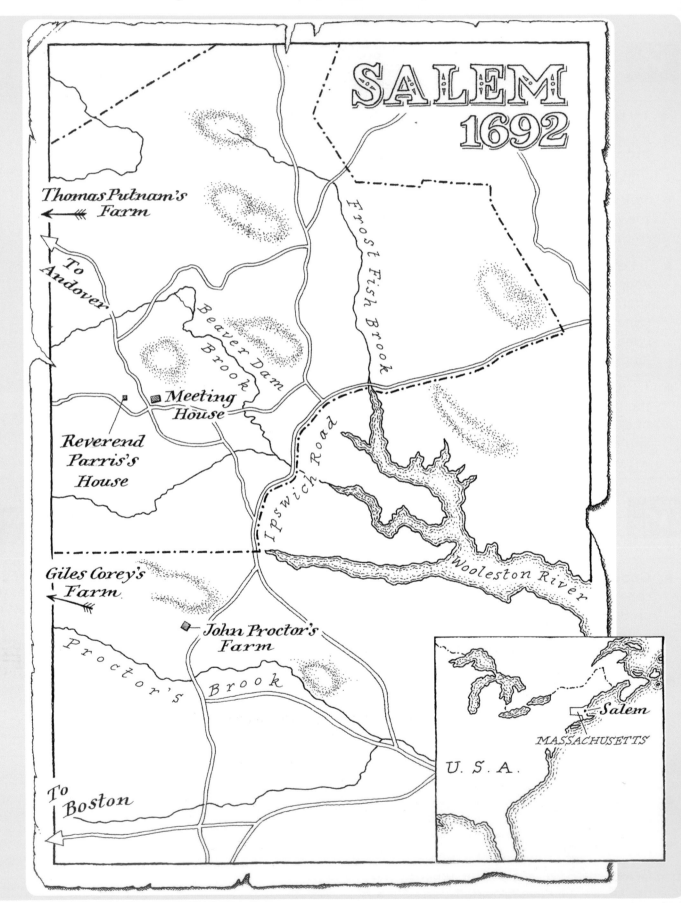

CHARACTERS: WHO'S WHO

Reverend Hale

Abigail Williams

Reverend Parris

Rebecca Nurse

John & Elizabeth Proctor

Giles Corey

Thomas & Ann Putnam

Tituba

Mary Warren

ARTHUR MILLER: AUTHOR AND CONTEXT

1915	Arthur Miller is born in New York
1934–38	Studies at the University of Michigan
1939–45	Second World War
1949	*Death of a Salesman* premieres
1950	Senator Joseph McCarthy begins his campaign against Communism in the US State Department
1953	*The Crucible* opens
1954	Marries film star Marilyn Monroe
1957	Convicted of contempt of Congress for failing to name possible US Communists
1961	Divorces Marilyn Monroe; *The Misfits*, a film, premieres
2005	Arthur Miller dies on 10 February

PART TWO: PLOT AND ACTION

Plot summary: What happens in *The Crucible*?

REVISION ACTIVITY

- Go through the summary lists below and **highlight** what you think is the **key moment** in each part of the play.
- Then find each moment in the **text** and **re-read** it. Write down **two reasons** why you think each moment is so **important**.

ACT ONE

- In Salem, 1692, some girls have been caught dancing in the forest.
- The younger girls are frightened and pretend to be ill.
- The town's minister, Parris, is worried that word will get out that his daughter Betty and his niece Abigail were among the girls. He is worried for his reputation.
- The Putnams arrive at Parris's house and are pleased to find that the minister's daughter is ill.
- They jump to witchcraft as an explanation.
- This suits the Putnams as they are interested in revenge on their neighbours, including Parris who was appointed to the position that a relation of the Putnams wanted.
- John Proctor is left alone with Abigail and she tries to rekindle the affair she had with him when she was the servant in his house.
- He refuses her advances and she loses her temper, mentioning that she blames his wife, Elizabeth.
- Betty wakes up and screams, bringing the others back into the room.
- Reverend Hale, a famous witch-finder, arrives and begins to look for signs of witchcraft in Betty Parris.
- When Abigail is asked about the dancing and conjuring in the forest she blames the black slave, Tituba, who she says bewitched her.

- Tituba is questioned by Hale and quickly becomes confused. She merely repeats whatever suggestion is put to her and ends up confessing to having dealt with the Devil.
- Abigail joins in with the confession and both girls call out the names of people whom they have seen with the Devil.

ACT TWO

- Eight days later, the Proctors' servant, Mary Warren, has become an official of the court appointed to look into the rumours of witchcraft.
- Many more people have now been accused.
- Elizabeth wants her husband to go to the court and denounce Abigail, who is clearly behind the accusations. Proctor reluctantly agrees to go. Mary Warren returns and brings Elizabeth a 'poppet'.
- Shortly afterwards, Hale arrives and questions the Proctors as to the Christian nature of their home.
- Officials from the court bring a warrant for the arrest of Elizabeth, and they have been instructed to search the house for 'poppets'.

- They find such a doll with a needle stuck in its stomach.
- This resembles the way that Abigail found herself to be stabbed with a needle that same evening.
- Elizabeth is arrested.

ACT THREE

- Giles Corey goes to court to try to save his own wife.
- Proctor arrives to present evidence that Abigail and the girls have been lying all along.
- He has persuaded Mary Warren to tell the truth about the girls but she is very nervous at the prospect.
- When Danforth, the deputy-governor, seems to doubt Abigail (on the testimony of Mary Warren), Abigail pretends that Mary is sending her spirit out to attack her.
- Proctor stops this by confessing that he had an affair with Abigail and says that the girl is simply trying to kill his wife out of jealousy.
- Elizabeth Proctor is brought in and questioned.
- Elizabeth defends her husband's good name, even though she does know of his affair.
- Hale believes Proctor, and Danforth begins to listen to reason.
- Abigail screams that she is being attacked by a bird sent by Mary Warren.
- The girls join her in crying out against Mary.
- This frightens Mary so much that she sides with Abigail and says that Proctor is the Devil's man.
- Proctor is arrested and Hale denounces the court, realising that justice has not been done.

ACT FOUR

- Tituba and Sarah Good are to be hanged.
- Reverend Hale tries to persuade the accused to confess rather than hang.
- We learn that Abigail has run off with Parris's money.
- There are rumours of rebellion against the trials.
- Parris is frightened for his life.
- John Proctor is given a last chance to confess to witchcraft and so save his life.
- He is allowed to speak to his wife and decides that he will confess.
- Proctor refuses to allow his signed confession to be posted on the door of the church.
- Proctor chooses to die rather than give up his good name.

Act One

Pages 1–5: An overture

Summary

❶ The character of Reverend Parris is introduced.

❷ We hear about the town of Salem and its inhabitants.

❸ We learn that the play will be about a witch-hunt.

Why is this section important?

A Miller provides us with detailed **historical background** to the play.

B We learn about the **tensions** and disagreements in the town.

C **Reverend Parris** is described.

D We are ready to learn how the 'tragedy' (p. 4) will **unfold**.

> **KEY QUOTE**
>
> 'The edge of the wilderness was close by … It stood, dark and threatening, over their shoulders night and day.' (p. 3)

Life in Salem

After describing the room in Parris's home, Miller supplies some background information about the small town of Salem, Massachusetts.

Salem had been in existence for only forty years. Life in the small town was hard, and the strict religious code made it harder by forbidding any form of 'vain enjoyment' (p. 2) such as the theatre, singing or dancing.

People were expected to attend worship and there were special wardens appointed to take down the names of those who did not attend so that the magistrates could be informed.

The land bordering Salem was largely unexplored, 'dark and threatening' (p. 3), and wild animals, along with marauding Indian tribes, posed a constant threat. This made many people conform to strict rules that they might otherwise have ignored.

REASONS FOR THE WITCH-HUNT

Salem was governed through a combination of state and religious power, 'a theocracy' (p. 4), in the hope of keeping evil at bay. As the times became less dangerous, the need for such strict rules lessened and people began to express an interest in 'greater individual freedom' (p. 5). The witch-hunt came about as people began to explore this freedom.

The witch-hunt also gave people 'a long overdue opportunity' (p. 5) to revenge themselves upon old enemies and to settle old scores to do with land ownership. Some people used it as a way to free their consciences from sins they had committed, by blaming things upon innocent victims.

> **? DID YOU KNOW**
>
> Many people fled to America to escape religious persecution back in England and so the Puritan lifestyle was fiercely guarded.

EXAMINER'S TIP: WRITING ABOUT REVEREND PARRIS

Miller tells us about Reverend Parris's position in the community and about his relationships with its members:

> In history he cut a villainous path, and there is very little good to be said for him. He believed he was being persecuted wherever he went, despite his best efforts to win people and God to his side. (p. 1)

We are told that he is an intolerant man who is quick to take offence and feels he is not shown the respect due to him as minister. It is important to bear these things in mind when considering Reverend Parris's behaviour in the next section.

Pages 5–14: Betty is taken ill

SUMMARY

DID YOU KNOW

Even devoutly religious people like Parris kept slaves during this period.

❶ Parris prays for his daughter Betty, who has fallen ill.

❷ Tituba, his black slave, enters. Parris brought her with him from Barbados where he used to be a merchant. Tituba is frightened by Betty's sudden fit.

❸ Parris's niece, Abigail, enters and tells him that Susanna Walcott, a servant, has come with news from the doctor.

❹ The doctor has suggested that there could be supernatural causes for Betty's illness.

❺ Parris questions Abigail: he saw her dancing in the woods with Betty, and wants to know why she has been dismissed from Goody Proctor's service.

❻ The Putnams visit; their daughter Ruth is sick too.

❼ Mercy Lewis, the Putnams' servant, arrives with news of Ruth. She says that Ruth has shown signs of improving.

❽ The Putnams leave with Parris, who has gone to pray with the crowd outside.

❾ Abigail and Mercy are left alone with Betty.

★ GRADE BOOSTER

The Putnams are delighted that Parris is in trouble. They might be able to replace him as minister and blame their own misfortunes on witchcraft at the same time. The Putnams deviously manipulate the situation for their own ends. Think about the ways people use this crisis for their own purposes in the play.

WHY IS THIS SECTION IMPORTANT?

A We see how seriously **witchcraft** is regarded in Salem and how people **fear** the Devil.

B Reverend Parris is **worried** about Betty but also about how his **enemies** in the community might use this event **against him**. Indeed, the Putnams arrive and add to his fears.

C We learn of the dancing in the forest and **questions** are raised about the **reputation** of Parris's niece Abigail.

THE SUPERNATURAL: FEAR AND DENIAL

When Susanna says that the doctor can find no explanation for Betty's illness in his books, but that Parris 'might look to unnatural things for the cause of it' (p. 7), Parris is frightened and angered. He is already unpopular in the town and he knows that he cannot afford to be associated with any suggestion of unnatural events. Parris is shown as a miserable, harsh man who thinks that everyone else should be as serious as he is. This extends even to young children, whom Parris does not understand at all. He turns on Abigail and confronts her with the fact that he caught her, Betty and others dancing in the forest. Abigail admits to this but says 'when you leaped out of the bush so suddenly, Betty was frightened and then she fainted' (p. 7). When Parris caught the girls, Tituba was with them. Tituba was waving her arms, screeching and swaying over the fire.

CHECKPOINT 1

Do you think that the involvement of Tituba and Abigail differs from that of the other girls?

Despite Parris's accusations of witchcraft, Abigail tells him that 'It were sport, uncle!' (p. 8). She knows she is close to being found out and tries to claim the girls' activities were innocent. Parris thinks he saw someone naked running through the trees, but Abigail denies this.

SLAVERY AND PREJUDICE

Parris asks his niece why she was dismissed from Goody Proctor's service and why Goody Proctor says she will not come to church if it means sitting near something so soiled as Abigail. She replies that she was treated like a slave by Mrs Proctor and 'will not black my face for any of them!' (p. 9), meaning that she will not be treated in the way that slaves from Barbados, like Tituba, are treated. Abigail loses her temper and calls Goody Proctor 'a gossiping liar' (p. 9). Parris is very close to discovering the real reason that Abigail left the Proctors' house. He is put off from doing so by the arrival of the Putnams.

THE PUTNAMS ARE EXCITED BY THE SCANDAL

Arthur Miller tells us that the Putnams resent Parris and are deeply vengeful people. Thomas Putnam had opposed the appointment of the previous minister as he wanted his own brother-in-law to have the position. This resentment is carried over to Parris.

When Mrs Putnam enters, she is pleased that misfortune has befallen Parris. She has heard that Betty flew over Ingersoll's barn. Before Parris can refute this, Thomas Putnam enters. He ignores the minister and goes straight to the bed to look at Betty. He compares Betty with his own daughter, who has also been taken ill. Mrs Putnam says that the girls are not merely sick, but that 'it's death drivin' into them, forked and hoofed' (p. 10).

Despite Parris's denial that any witchcraft has taken place, he has sent for Reverend Hale of Beverly, a well-known expert in the 'demonic arts' (p. 10). Putnam sees this as an admission of the minister's guilt and says that the village must know of it. Mrs Putnam says that she lost seven babies shortly after their birth, and that her only child has been strange recently. Because of this she sent her daughter, Ruth, to see Tituba, believing that the slave has magic powers.

It is really Mrs Putnam's actions that lead to the suggestion of witchcraft. She does not see that her daughter was simply becoming an adolescent, but prefers to blame Ruth's change in behaviour on her having been bewitched. Note her continuous alternation between rational and hysterical remarks.

EXAMINER'S TIP: WRITING ABOUT THE GIRLS 🔓

The girls are involved in various ways:

- Abigail is the strongest character and dominates the others, who are generally frightened of her.

- Tituba's African culture has made their games seem more exciting, and she becomes terrified of the consequences.

KEY QUOTE

Mrs Putnam: 'Tituba knows how to speak to the dead, Mr Parris.' (p. 12)

KEY CONNECTION

The Chrysalids by John Wyndham (1955) is set in a future when any differences or mutations in plants, animals or humans are seen as works of the Devil.

GLOSSARY

forked and hooved the Devil was often thought to have a forked tail and cloven hooves

Pages 14–17: Abigail, Mercy and Betty

Summary

❶ We learn what the girls have really been up to in the forest.

❷ Betty wakes up, feels threatened by Abigail and asks for her (dead) mother. She then tries to climb out of the window but is pulled back by Abigail, who hits her.

❸ Abigail also threatens Mercy and Mary Warren, John Proctor's servant.

❹ We learn that Abigail hates John Proctor's wife.

❺ John Proctor's arrival brings an end to their argument.

Why is this section important?

A The girls are frightened of **punishment**, and this **fear** makes them desperate to find ways out of the situation.

B It turns out that there were sinister **motives** behind some of their behaviour: Abigail is driven by hatred of John Proctor's wife.

C We learn of Abigail's history and begin to see her **power** over the other girls.

Revelations

Mercy tells Abigail that Ruth's illness is 'weirdish' (p. 14). When Mercy offers to hit Betty to bring her round, Abigail holds her back and tells Mercy that she has admitted to dancing in the woods. She says that Parris 'knows Tituba conjured Ruth's sisters to come out of the grave' (p. 14). Mercy also finds out that Parris saw her naked. When Mary Warren, the servant of John Proctor, enters she wants to tell the adults what the girls were doing in the forest and says that Abigail will only be whipped for what they did. Abigail tells Mary that if she is whipped then Mary will be too.

Betty has heard Abigail talking to Parris and knows that she has not told him everything: 'You drank blood, Abby! You didn't tell him that!' (p. 15). Abigail did this in order to cast a spell to kill Proctor's wife. Abigail tells the girls that they are to admit to dancing and to conjuring Ruth's dead sisters but not to any of 'the other things' (p. 15). Mary Warren still wants them to own up to everything. Abigail is prevented from hitting her by the entrance of John Proctor.

Abigail's history

In this section we learn that Abigail has a very troubled past: 'I saw Indians smash my dear parents' heads on the pillow next to mine' (p. 15). This terrible experience seems to have hardened her and she threatens the other girls with violence.

KEY QUOTE

Abigail: 'I will come to you in the black of some terrible night and I will bring a pointy reckoning that will shudder you.' (p. 15)

EXAMINER'S TIP: WRITING ABOUT THE GIRLS' TRUE NATURES

Abigail and Mercy are genuinely puzzled and concerned by Betty and Ruth's condition. They have not yet grasped the seriousness of the situation. Remember that they are still quite young and have not yet become a part of adult society.

Abigail clearly frightens the other girls and they are prepared to do whatever she tells them. Abigail is obviously the ringleader and shows that she is able to keep her head in a difficult situation, while Mary is described as 'a subservient, naive, lonely girl' (p. 14).

Think about the girls' lives in the village and why they have been up to mischief in the woods.

CHECKPOINT 2

In what way is Abigail still rather innocent here?

Pages 16–19: Abigail and Proctor

SUMMARY

❶ Abigail is alone with Proctor, probably for the first time since their affair.

❷ Abigail wants to continue the affair but Proctor rejects her.

❸ Abigail quickly turns against her former lover.

❹ The sound of a psalm is heard from outside, and Betty sits up and calls out.

❺ The noise she makes brings Parris back into the room.

WHY IS THIS SECTION IMPORTANT?

A John Proctor appears to be a **level-headed** and **independent** man.

B Abigail's **motives** become clearer.

C John Proctor shows a strong **moral sense** and is determined to put past **weaknesses** behind him.

D We see that **Proctor's wife** stands in **Abigail's way**.

A STRONG MAN?

John Proctor is in his mid-thirties and is a well-respected farmer. He is known for being strong and people are wary of him. Proctor scolds Mary for neglecting her duties and sends her home. Mercy Lewis also leaves, saying that she has to look after Ruth; Miller tells us that she is 'both afraid of him and strangely titillated' (p. 17). Abigail immediately flatters Proctor: 'Gah! I'd almost forgot how strong you are, John Proctor!' (p. 17). He has heard the rumours of witchcraft, and Abigail says that it is all because her uncle caught her and some other girls dancing in the forest the night before. Proctor seems to encourage Abigail: 'Ah, you're wicked yet, aren't y'!' (p. 17).

> **KEY QUOTE**
>
> '… it is a man in his prime we see, with a quiet confidence and an unexpressed, hidden force.' (p. 16)

ABIGAIL'S DESPERATION

When Abigail tries to seduce Proctor, saying 'I am waitin' for you every night' (p. 17), he tells her that he never gave her such hope. She replies that she has more than hope and refers to her affair with him. Abigail condemns Proctor's wife for the end of the affair and says that she knows Proctor has been thinking of her.

Abigail clutches Proctor and he gently moves her aside. As he does so he calls her 'Child' (p. 18). This angers Abigail, who tells him that, thanks to him, she is no longer a child. Abigail vows to act against Elizabeth Proctor, whom she calls 'a cold, snivelling woman' (p. 19). Proctor tries to leave, but Abigail rushes to him and begs him to take pity on her.

EXAMINER'S TIP: WRITING ABOUT THE END OF THE AFFAIR

Abigail's continued attraction to Proctor is one of the key driving forces behind events. They have had an affair and still feel a strong physical attraction for each other, as Abigail declares:

> you loved me then and you do now! (p. 18)

Proctor, however, has made up his mind that the affair with Abigail is over, and he shows strength of character in refusing her:

> … I will cut off my hand before I'll ever reach for you again. (p. 18)

Abigail naturally feels abandoned by Proctor. It is now that bitterness sets in, and she begins to seek vengeance.

Think about what you learned in the previous section about Abigail's parents. Does this make her relationship with Proctor, and the end of the affair, all the more significant?

CHECKPOINT 3

How does Abigail's behaviour change when Proctor enters the room?

CHECKPOINT 4

How might Proctor be said to have behaved badly towards Abigail?

GLOSSARY

titillated excited, possibly in a sexual way

Pages 19–26: Small-town politics

SUMMARY

❶ Parris rushes to Betty's side.

❷ The Putnams arrive and make the situation worse.

❸ Rebecca Nurse enters and Parris asks her to help Betty.

❹ Giles Corey appears and asks whether Betty is going to fly again.

❺ Rebecca Nurse, an old woman of the parish, calms Betty.

❻ We learn about the feud between the Nurses and the Putnams.

❼ Parris's preaching comes under criticism from John Proctor.

❽ Parris and Proctor voice their grievances, attacking each other, and Giles joins in against Putnam.

CHECKPOINT 5

What do we learn here about Giles Corey?

WHY IS THIS SECTION IMPORTANT?

A There is more evidence of factions and **enmities** within the community.

B We see that Rebecca Nurse is a **kind** and **sensible** woman.

C Some of the disputes in Salem concern **money** and **land**.

DIFFERENT RESPONSES TO BETTY'S ILLNESS

It is a coincidence that Betty has cried out while a prayer was being said, but Mrs Putnam says that the girl cannot bear to hear the Lord's name. Thomas Putnam adds, 'That is a notorious sign of witchcraft afoot' (p. 20). Husband and wife seem delighted to be able to point the finger of suspicion at Parris.

Rebecca says that Betty will be fine if everyone leaves her alone. She knows that the little girl is frightened and looking for attention. Proctor backs her in this and challenges Parris over the fact that he has sent for Reverend Hale. Proctor also argues with Putnam and says that the town should have been consulted before this step was taken: 'This society will not be a bag to swing around your head, Mr Putnam' (p. 22).

Proctor is quick to see that Putnam is using the situation to try to further his own cause. His predictions of Putnam's intentions are frighteningly accurate, as we see later how the Putnams profit from the witchcraft trials. Putnam retorts by saying that Proctor has not been seen at church for some time. Proctor claims that this is because he will not listen to the 'hellfire and bloody damnation' (p. 23) preached by Parris. Rebecca supports this allegation.

? DID YOU KNOW

Not being able to bear to listen to prayer was thought to be a clear sign of being in league with the Devil.

DISCORD IN THE PARISH

When Parris complains that the people of Salem do not respect him and brings up the fact that he has not been supplied with firewood, Giles and Proctor remind him that he is paid a salary of £60 and given £6 more for firewood. Proctor also complains that Parris keeps asking for the deeds to the minister's house. Later, when Parris says that there is a faction in Salem opposed to him, Proctor adds that he would like to join such a faction.

By setting himself against Parris at this early stage, Proctor unwittingly gives Parris and Putnam reasons to arrest him later on. It is important that the dispute between Giles and Putnam is over land and that Putnam threatens to take Corey to court. Giles has a reputation for filing law suits and has even had Proctor fined recently. He says too much against Putnam here and so seals his fate.

EXAMINER'S TIP: WRITING ABOUT THE FEUDING FAMILIES

There is a complex web of relationships and feuds in the parish of Salem. In this section Miller tells us about the history of the Nurses and the Putnams. Understanding this history will help you to write about the characters' motivations:

- The Nurses had been involved in long-running disputes over land with a member of the Putnam family.

- It was the Nurse family who had prevented Putnam's brother-in-law from becoming minister. The Nurses had established their own township outside Salem and this was deeply resented by Putnam.

- The first complaint against Rebecca Nurse was signed by Edward and Jonathan Putnam, and it was Ruth Putnam who pointed out Rebecca, in the courtroom, as her attacker.

Arthur Miller drew on the records of the real Salem witchcraft trials when writing this play.

CHECKPOINT 6

What do Parris's complaints reveal about his character?

CHECKPOINT 7

How does Rebecca Nurse manage to cure Betty so easily?

Pages 26–40: Reverend John Hale

SUMMARY

❶ Hale arrives and prepares to drive out the Devil from Betty.

❷ Giles Corey says too much and endangers his own wife.

❸ Hale questions Abigail, who nearly cracks but mentions Tituba.

❹ Tituba gets the blame and, under interrogation by Hale, begins naming witches.

❺ Abigail and Betty join in.

WHY IS THIS SECTION IMPORTANT?

A Reverend Hale is greeted as an **expert** in witchcraft and raises **hopes** that the situation will be resolved.

B We see that some of the people are extremely **superstitious**. Mrs Putnam believes she has lost children through witchcraft.

C Abigail **copies** Tituba and begins to name people as possible witches. She sees how powerful **fear** and **hysteria** can be.

CHECKPOINT 8

How is there a sign here that Mrs Putnam will later bring trouble to Rebecca Nurse?

THE EXPERT

Hale is introduced, and in his long introduction Miller draws parallels with the situation in America during the McCarthy era (see **Key Contexts**). Hale believes himself to be an educated witch-finder. He thinks that he has all the Devil's ways accounted for in his books and sees the people of Salem as naive in their interpretations of evil.

Hale takes the proceedings very seriously: 'He feels himself allied with the best minds of Europe' (p. 30). He is told the symptoms of Betty and Ruth, and Proctor says that he hopes Hale will bring some sense to the situation. Hale reprimands Putnam for saying that being unable to bear to hear the Lord's name is a sure sign of witchcraft. Hale points out 'We cannot look to superstition in this' (p. 31), making it clear that only he has the power to make a judgement.

Hale is surprised to hear that the townsfolk allow dancing, and Mrs Putnam tells him that Tituba was engaged in magic. She is adamant that it was not natural for her to lose seven children in childbirth. Rebecca Nurse is 'horrified', saying 'Goody Ann! You sent a child to conjure up the dead?' (p. 32). It is significant that Rebecca leaves, quietly refusing to have anything to do with the proceedings.

When Hale prepares to exorcise the Devil from Betty, Giles Corey interrupts and begins to ask questions about his own wife. Giles claims that his wife reads strange books and that this has stopped Giles from praying. Hale ignores him and concentrates on Betty, praying over her in Latin. Betty does not stir.

ABIGAIL UNDER PRESSURE

Hale questions Abigail as to what the girls were doing in the forest. Parris adds that he thinks he might have seen a kettle in the grass. When Hale asks him if there had been any movement in the kettle, Parris says that there was. Abigail denies full participation but mentions Tituba, who is then sent for. Hale enquires as to whether Abigail had felt a cold wind or a trembling below the ground. Parris and Abigail take up Hale's suggestions. They hope that by agreeing with Hale suspicion might be lifted from them. When Hale presses Abigail, she insists 'I'm a good girl! I'm a proper girl!' (p. 35). However, Abigail commits to memory much of the information about witchcraft that is given here. She will use this later, especially in the court scene.

INTERROGATION

Tituba is brought in and Abigail accuses her of making her 'do it' (p. 35). She says that Tituba makes her drink blood, and the slave admits to giving the girls chicken blood. Abigail blames her wicked dreams on Tituba, and Hale tells the slave to wake Betty. Putnam threatens to have Tituba hanged and, as a result, Tituba is terrified and clearly willing to say whatever she thinks the men want to hear. In fact, most of what Tituba says is at the prompting of Parris, Putnam and Hale. This grows more pronounced as the interrogation goes on and she simply repeats the last thing that is said to her. Tituba mixes her feelings for Parris and her desire to return to Barbados with her statements about the Devil. She is clearly very confused, but the men are too excited to notice.

Hale asks Tituba if the Devil came alone or with someone whom she recognised. Putnam asks if he came with Sarah Good or Osburn. Parris presses her as to whether it was a man or a woman who came, and Tituba says that they were all witches out of Salem. Hale tells Tituba that she has confessed and so can be forgiven. She says that four people came with the Devil and that the Devil tried to get her to kill Parris. Tituba names one of the people as Goody Osburn. Mrs Putnam seizes upon this information as Goody Osburn was her midwife three times.

CHECKPOINT 9

Why are the names suggested to Tituba important?

EXAMINER'S TIP: WRITING ABOUT THE POWER OF HYSTERIA

At this point in the play, some of the characters are terrified while others are quick to exploit this fear for their own ends. Abigail, as though she is in a trance, adds the names of Sarah Good and Bridget Bishop to the list – the two young women suggested by Putnam earlier. Notice how the whole idea of naming townsfolk starts here and begins to snowball. Betty simply becomes carried away; she cries out the names of George Jacobs and Goody Howe. Abigail uses this to divert attention from her own activities, realising the effect that strong emotions can have on a group of weak-minded people. It is here that she witnesses the unusual behaviour of several people who are carried along on a tide of hysteria, and it is clear that her later actions in Act Three reflect this new knowledge. Miller is using the situation both to show Abigail's cunning and as an **allegory** of the hysteria created during the McCarthy era.

CHECKPOINT 10

What dangerous ideas is Abigail able to pick up here?

Act Two

Pages 41–5: John and Elizabeth Proctor

SUMMARY

❶ It is eight days later in the Proctors' house.

❷ The relationship between John and Elizabeth Proctor has become strained.

❸ Mary Warren is attending the trials in court.

❹ There are now fourteen people in jail, who will be hanged if they do not confess.

❺ Elizabeth urges her husband to go to Salem and denounce the girls as liars.

❻ Proctor knows that Abigail's testimony is false but is reluctant to challenge her and the other girls in court as he fears that he will be exposed as an adulterer.

❼ Proctor loses his temper with Elizabeth, but he knows she is right.

KEY QUOTE

Elizabeth: 'I do not judge you. The magistrate sits in your heart that judges you.' (p. 45)

CHECKPOINT 11

How are John and Elizabeth Proctor affected by Abigail?

WHY IS THIS SECTION IMPORTANT?

A We witness the **tension** between John and Elizabeth Proctor.

B We hear about the **progress** of the witchcraft **investigations** in Salem **before** we **witness** the proceedings on stage.

C John Proctor is torn between **exposing** the girls and losing his **good name** in the community.

D We see the **great** struggle within Proctor as he is put under pressure by Elizabeth to go to court.

AN UNHAPPY MARRIAGE

The stage instructions say that Proctor is not pleased with the food in the pot over the fire and that he meddles with it. This behaviour indicates that he and Elizabeth are not getting on as well as they might. Throughout the opening sequence, the Proctors are distant from each other. They speak of the farm and the weather, but do not seem comfortable together. Miller's stage directions clearly show the awkwardness between the couple:

PROCTOR (*with a grin*): I mean to please you, Elizabeth.
ELIZABETH – (*it is hard to say*): I know it, John.

He gets up, goes to her, kisses her. She receives it. With a certain disappointment, he returns to the table. (p. 42)

GRADE BOOSTER

John Proctor's guilty conscience and his concern for his good name are central to the drama. Put yourself in Proctor's shoes and make a list of pros and cons for his going straight to the courthouse to say what he knows.

NEWS OF THE COURT

Mary Warren has been in Salem all day. This is against John Proctor's orders, but Mary is 'an official of the court' (p. 43) trying people for witchcraft, and so Elizabeth has let her go.

Elizabeth comments upon Abigail's new power and fame, saying 'where she walks the crowd will part like the sea for Israel' (p. 43). If Abigail and the girls scream and fall to the floor when someone is brought in front of them, that person is 'clapped in the jail' (p. 44).

EXAMINER'S TIP: WRITING ABOUT JOHN PROCTOR'S DILEMMA

Proctor cannot go to the court at this point as he would have to admit to his affair with Abigail and so blacken his name. He regrets having confessed his affair to Elizabeth. He realises that he has probably made a mistake in doing so; she has judged him harshly and it has driven a wedge between them. You could consider how much power Proctor has to change events at this stage, and how his disgust at his guilt later proves fatal in the court scene.

GLOSSARY

part like the sea for Israel in the Book of Exodus in the Bible, Moses parted the Red Sea to allow the Israelites to escape from Egypt

Pages 46–51: Mary Warren returns

SUMMARY

CHECKPOINT 12

What is important about the 'poppet'?

❶ Mary returns from court and Proctor is furious with her.

❷ Mary behaves strangely – she appears upset and shaken.

❸ She has brought Elizabeth a 'poppet', a *'small rag doll'* (p. 46), that she has made.

❹ Mary tells them that thirty-nine people have now been arrested, including Goody Osburn, who will be hanged.

❺ Mary also tells them that Sarah Good has been arrested after Mary accused her of bewitching her, and that Sarah has 'confessed'.

❻ Proctor threatens to whip Mary but she stands up to him.

❼ She tells them that someone has accused Elizabeth of being involved in the witchcraft.

❽ Elizabeth is convinced that Abigail means to see her hanged.

KEY QUOTE

Mary: 'she [Susan] sometimes made a compact with Lucifer, and wrote her name in his black book –' (p. 47)

WHY IS THIS SECTION IMPORTANT?

A We learn about the **power** the girls have shown in court. Even timid Mary feels **bold** enough to answer back to her employer Proctor.

B The court is already passing death sentences, which raises **fear** in the community.

C Elizabeth is now in **danger**.

D We are hearing about these events second hand, and this builds up **tension** and **anticipation** in the audience.

GRADE BOOSTER

Behind her new-found bravery, Mary is still terrified of Abigail and lacks the strength to stand up to her. When you are writing about the characters in the play, the examiner will be impressed if you show that each individual has different sides to their character.

A CHANGE IN MARY WARREN

Mary Warren is starting to lose her shyness as she begins to feel that she is important to the court. She has caught the communal hysteria and is embroidering fact with fantasy when she talks of Sarah Good. For the first time in her life Mary finds that adults will listen to her and treat her with respect. This goes to her head.

IS ELIZABETH TO BE NEXT?

When Proctor loses his temper and threatens to whip Mary, she stops him by saying that she saved Elizabeth's life in court that day. Elizabeth has been accused but Mary will not say by whom. Mary tells Proctor that he must 'speak civilly' (p. 49) to her and that she will not be ordered around by him. We have seen Proctor to be a strong and confident man, but he is now being defied by his previously timid servant girl.

Elizabeth feels sure that she will be proclaimed a witch by Abigail: 'She wants me dead' (p. 50). She asks Proctor to tell Abigail that he no longer feels anything for the girl and he reluctantly agrees.

CHECKPOINT 13

What do you learn about Abigail in this section?

EXAMINER'S TIP: WRITING ABOUT VENGEANCE

The treatment in court of Sarah Good is an indication of the fate that is to befall Proctor. Mary feels that 'it's God's work we do' (p. 49), but Proctor points out that hanging old women is 'strange work for a Christian girl' (p. 48).

We see that there are personal motives behind the girls' accusations and it is clear to Elizabeth not only who has denounced her but why: Abigail is jealous of Elizabeth, and having been rejected by Proctor now wants revenge on them both:

> ELIZABETH: She has an arrow in you yet, John Proctor, and you know it well!
>
> (pp. 51–2)

GLOSSARY

Lucifer
the Devil; the name means 'bringer of light', and Lucifer was the brightest angel in Heaven before he was cast out for being too proud

Pages 52–8: Hale and the Proctors

SUMMARY

❶ Hale appears in the Proctors' doorway.

❷ He says he is visiting the homes of people who have been accused.

❸ He questions John Proctor and Elizabeth about their religious beliefs and practices.

❹ Proctor explains his dislike of Reverend Parris and his golden candlesticks.

❺ To his embarrassment, Proctor cannot remember one of the Commandments – the one about adultery.

❻ Proctor tells Hale about the girls' foolishness and how Parris found them dancing in the wood.

❼ Hale asks Proctor and Elizabeth whether they believe in witches at all.

? DID YOU KNOW

Puritans did not believe in decoration or ornament – especially in church. Parris is clearly vain and interested in his appearance.

WHY IS THIS SECTION IMPORTANT?

A Hale's arrival shows that the **investigation** is moving closer to the Proctors. John Proctor was hoping to keep out of it.

B Proctor's usual **confidence** falters under Hale's questioning.

C He hopes his **information** about the girls **dancing** in the woods will be enough to **clear** things up.

D At this point, Elizabeth, who is confident about her religion, seems safely **above suspicion**.

E Hale seems to **believe** the Proctors and we feel that they may be **safe**.

REVEREND HALE'S INVESTIGATION

Hale is already feeling guilty about his involvement in the court's proceedings and wants to form his own opinion of the people who have been named as witches. He has just come from Rebecca Nurse's house as she has been mentioned in the court, though she has not been charged as yet. (The Putnams are responsible for the accusations against Rebecca Nurse.)

Hale presses Proctor as to why only two of his three boys had been baptised, and Proctor says that he did not want Parris to lay his hands on his son. He has, however, helped with carpentry on the church and this impresses Hale.

By the end of this section, Hale seems to have been fully convinced that the Proctors are telling the truth about the girls' testimony. He believes strongly in witches. He has studied them in books and is an acknowledged expert, but has serious doubts about the present crisis in Salem.

THE IMPORTANCE OF RELIGION

When John Proctor agrees to make his statement in court, Hale asks the Proctors whether they believe in witches. Proctor says that he will not contradict the Bible, but Elizabeth insists otherwise: 'If you think that I am one, then I say there are none' (p. 57). Hale tells them to baptise their third child and go to church each Sunday and to appear solemn in their manner. This reminds us of the strict religious code of the time and how a person's good character depended on such things as church attendance.

EXAMINER'S TIP: WRITING ABOUT HALE'S CHANGE OF MIND

We see that Hale's own beliefs are shaken by what Proctor tells him about the girls. He is forced to face up to the fact that he has been taken in by them even though he has been present when some of the accused have confessed to witchcraft.

Notice how important Miller's stage directions are in conveying Hale's change of mind: '(It is his own suspicion but he resists it ...)' (p. 56), and later, '(quietly – it has impressed him)' (p. 57).

KEY QUOTE

Proctor: 'There are them that will swear to anything before they'll hang;' (p. 56)

CHECKPOINT 14

How does Proctor's information affect Hale?

Pages 58–66: Elizabeth is arrested

SUMMARY

❶ Giles Corey and Francis Nurse arrive with news that both their wives have been arrested.

❷ Rebecca Nurse has been charged with murdering Ann Putnam's babies.

❸ Hale still believes that he has seen some proof of witchcraft in court.

❹ Ezekiel Cheever and Marshall Herrick arrive with a warrant for Elizabeth's arrest.

❺ Cheever finds a 'poppet' with a needle stuck inside it.

❻ He reports that Abigail was found with a needle in her stomach earlier that night.

❼ Mary admits that she made the 'poppet' and that Abigail sat beside her.

❽ John takes the warrant from Cheever and rips it up.

❾ Elizabeth is arrested amid violence and confusion.

❿ John tells Mary that she must go to court and tell the truth, but she is terrified of Abigail.

⓫ John shakes her violently and says that they must tell the truth about Abigail.

WHY IS THIS SECTION IMPORTANT?

A The **pace** quickens in the drama with the news of more arrests.

B Hale still believes that things will be **sorted out** in court.

C Elizabeth's arrest forces John to take **active steps** to save her and **discredit** Abigail and the girls.

D The needle in the '**poppet**' is part of Abigail's plot against Elizabeth, but the **proof** depends on Mary Warren **testifying** against her in court.

ACCUSATIONS AND ARRESTS

Giles Corey's earlier accusations about his wife reading strange books have not helped her. People such as Mrs Putnam and Walcott are clearly using the court proceedings to carry out their private revenge upon their neighbours. Hale assures Nurse that the justice of the court will ensure that Rebecca will be released. Corey's wife has been charged by Walcott, Susanna's father. Walcott has had a dispute with Martha Corey over a pig he had bought from her. This seems a petty dispute but it has led to Martha's arrest.

THE TRUTH ABOUT THE 'POPPET'

Cheever has been instructed to search the house for 'poppets'. He sees one on the mantelpiece; it is Mary's, and she is sent for.

When Mary admits to putting the needle in the doll herself and says 'Ask Abby, Abby sat beside me when I made it' (p. 62), Hale suspects that this might not be her 'natural memory' (p. 62). He believes Mary might be under some kind of spell making her act against Abigail, but in fact the only evil influence at work is Abigail herself.

EXAMINER'S TIP

At this stage in the play, look at the way in which Abigail and the girls have fooled most of the town's adults. This will help you to comment on Abigail's character.

CHECKPOINT 15

What aspect of Hale's character is shown here?

DID YOU KNOW

The use of dolls to cast spells on people was thought to be a method used by witches. It is also connected with the voodoo that Tituba claims to practise.

Although they are not spelled out in this section, it is clear that the events surrounding the 'poppet' are as follows:

● Mary Warren was sewing a 'poppet' in court to pass the time as she was bored.

● She stuck the needle in the doll to keep it safe.

● Abigail saw Mary do this.

● During dinner at Parris's house, Abigail fell to the floor screaming and a needle was found stuck two inches into the flesh of her stomach.

● When the doll is examined by Cheever it is found to have a needle stuck in it.

It is clear to the reader that Abigail has watched Mary stick the needle in the 'poppet' and has later stabbed herself with a needle, knowing that by this time the doll will be in Elizabeth Proctor's house. She wants to revenge herself upon Elizabeth.

ELIZABETH'S ARREST: A TURNING POINT

Proctor says that the warrant for Elizabeth's arrest is simply 'vengeance' (p. 63). When Herrick chains Elizabeth, Proctor promises to 'pay' him for it (p. 64). Giles tells Hale to act, as Hale knows this is all fraud, but Hale says that there must be some cause for all the accusations.

When Proctor tells Mary that she must admit to the court how the 'poppet' came to be in his house, Mary is frightened and says that she cannot do it as Abigail would kill her and 'charge lechery' (p. 65) on Proctor. It is therefore through Elizabeth's arrest that Mary reveals that she knows of the affair. The Act closes with Mary weeping that she cannot do what Proctor has asked her. The power that Abigail has over the girls is clearly shown in Mary's terror at the prospect of having to denounce Abigail in court.

> **KEY QUOTE**
>
> Proctor: 'little crazy children are jangling the keys of the kingdom, and common vengeance writes the law!' (p. 63)

> **CHECKPOINT 16**
>
> Why do the men come to Proctor for help?

EXAMINER'S TIP: WRITING ABOUT CONFUSION

At this point in the play there is a great deal of confusion. The only characters who realise what is actually happening are the Proctors and Abigail. This is highly **ironic** as Abigail is now thinking of a way to hurt Elizabeth. The other characters are involved in different ways and for different reasons, but confusion reigns:

● Hale is confused at the Proctors' seemingly good characters and still believes the girls are telling the truth.

● The Putnams are exploiting the confusion in order to settle old scores.

● The judges firmly believe in the testimony of the girls and have allowed themselves to be tricked.

● The townsfolk are divided between wanting to stop the arrests and fearing the power of the court and the church.

● Mary Warren is so confused as to believe that she is actually doing good work in the court.

The audience is presented with several different viewpoints of the situation and is given little guidance as to who will win and how far the truth will be taken seriously.

Pages 79–96: Mary confronts the girls

SUMMARY

❶ Proctor presents new evidence from Mary, in which she admits that she has lied in court even though her evidence has condemned people to death.

❷ Hale realises the importance of Mary's words and requests that a lawyer is present. Danforth refuses.

❸ The girls are questioned and Abigail sticks firmly to her story.

❹ Proctor reveals that Parris saw the girls dancing in the wood and Hale confirms this, forcing Parris to admit to it.

❺ Mary is asked to pretend to faint and is unable to do so, but she maintains that it was all 'only sport in the beginning' (p. 86).

❻ Abigail is angry and threatens Danforth, but realises her mistake and pretends to feel a cold wind coming from Mary.

❼ Desperate, Proctor confesses to his adultery with Abigail and says that he confessed it to his wife.

❽ Elizabeth is brought into court but lies to protect Proctor's good name. Her lie condemns her husband.

❾ Abigail and the girls cause a distraction by claiming to see a yellow bird that Mary has conjured and possessed in order to injure them.

❿ Mary is overcome by the force of the girls' attack on her and falls back under Abigail's spell, renouncing Proctor.

⓫ Proctor is arrested and accused of being 'combined with anti-Christ' (p. 96).

⓬ Hale denounces the court and leaves.

KEY QUOTE

Proctor: 'She thinks to dance with me on my wife's grave!' (p. 89)

WHY IS THIS SECTION IMPORTANT?

A We want to know what effect Mary's evidence will have and whether she is strong enough to stick to her story. This creates **tension**.

B Everyone is under **pressure**: even Parris is forced into a **confession**.

C The end of the Act is full of **incident** and **drama**, particularly in Proctor's confession of adultery and Elizabeth's **error**.

D Abigail is clever enough to cause a diversion. We see how **cunning** and **powerful** she is.

GRADE BOOSTER

Think about how Danforth's reactions affect the dramatic tension in this section.

PARRIS IS UNCOMFORTABLE

Proctor tells Danforth that the girls were caught dancing in the woods and Danforth begins to question Parris about this. Parris is desperate to keep his family out of the revelations about the dancing in the forest, but he cannot. He is not interested in justice, merely in saving his own name. Danforth is clearly becoming more and more suspicious of Parris as he finds out about the girls' antics in the forest but, crucially, he fails to act.

ELIZABETH'S FATAL ERROR

Elizabeth lies to protect her husband by denying all knowledge of the affair between Proctor and Abigail. It is an example of dramatic irony that Elizabeth, a woman who supposedly never lies, tells this untruth and ends up condemning her husband as a liar and making Abigail seem believable once more. She realises too late that she should have told the truth, and she is led away. Hale still believes Proctor as he feels that Elizabeth's statement 'is a natural lie to tell' (p. 91).

Here Elizabeth has lied to save her husband's reputation. Even a lie told with good intent can have a destructive effect. Later, Proctor is urged by Hale to lie to save his life. The truth is shown to be more powerful than lies in both cases.

THE 'YELLOW BIRD' EPISODE

Abigail's power is once more evident as she goes on to control the girls psychologically just as much as she did physically in Act One. The other girls soon join Abigail in mimicking Mary, and we see both the power of the imagination and peer pressure at work here.

EXAMINER'S TIP: WRITING ABOUT THE TRIAL

This is one of the most dramatic passages in the play. Try to identify the parts where it seems possible that John Proctor might win and where things turn against him: for example, when Danforth is prepared to listen to Proctor and his two friends, and when he starts to question Parris about the dancing in the woods. The truth is nearly uncovered after John's painful confession, but Abigail always manages to turn things in her favour. Look at how she uses things she has picked up, such as the 'cold wind' and the Devil, which Reverend Hale had mentioned in Act One. How important are each of these factors in influencing the trial?

- Abigail's power over the girls
- the general superstition in Salem
- the judges' fear of looking foolish.

CHECKPOINT 19

Why does Abigail pretend to be attacked once again?

CHECKPOINT 20

Where does Abigail nearly go too far?

GLOSSARY

anti-Christ the opposite to Christ, i.e. the Devil

Act Four

Pages 97–116: Day of execution

SUMMARY

❶ Sarah Good and Tituba are removed from the jail cell by Marshall Herrick.

❷ Parris tells Danforth and Hathorne that Abigail has disappeared with his money.

❸ Parris is frightened by rumours that the trials are causing unrest in the area. He urges Hathorne and Danforth to delay the executions of Proctor and Rebecca Nurse: 'You cannot hang this sort. There is danger for me' (p. 103).

❹ Danforth refuses to delay the hangings.

❺ Reverend Hale has been begging prisoners to confess and save their lives.

❻ Danforth and Hale urge Elizabeth to persuade Proctor to confess. She agrees to talk to him.

❼ Proctor says he is prepared to confess and live.

❽ Rebecca Nurse refuses to confess.

❾ Proctor changes his mind and refuses to have his confession displayed on the church door.

❿ Elizabeth watches Proctor's execution from the cell window.

CHECKPOINT 21

Why do you think Abigail has disappeared?

KEY QUOTE

Elizabeth: 'He have his goodness now. God forbid I take it from him!' (p. 116)

WHY IS THIS SECTION IMPORTANT?

A We are reminded that many of the **victims** are poor and **weak** like Tituba and Sarah Good.

B We hear that people in the district are beginning to **turn against** the court, and Abigail, probably fearing **exposure**, has fled with Mercy Lewis.

C Hale is shown to be a broken **guilt-ridden** man.

D John Proctor chooses to die for the truth and his good **reputation**.

PATHETIC VICTIMS

This episode with Tituba and Sarah shows us how bewildered and powerless people were often the first victims of the trials. Tituba tries to escape through fantasy and Sarah through drink. This helps to undermine the dignity of the proceedings in our view.

FEARS OF REBELLION

The consequences of the trials are causing a reaction. Cattle are wandering loose, farms are neglected and some of the accused have a great deal of support in the community. Parris says, 'many honest people will weep for them' (p. 102), but he is only concerned for his own skin. He found a dagger outside his door. Hathorne and Danforth refuse to back down. Things have gone too far: 'There will be no postponement' (p. 102).

JOHN PROCTOR'S CONFESSION

Proctor decides to confess as he will then be able to look after his family. He does not feel worthy enough to die heroically. However, he will only confess to his own guilt and refuses to name others. When faced with Rebecca Nurse, who will not confess to witchcraft, he becomes ashamed. He signs the confession but tears it up when he hears it is to be put on public display: 'I have given you my soul; leave me my name!' (p. 115).

EXAMINER'S TIP: WRITING ABOUT MOTIVES AND PRESSURES 🔓

Think about the conflicting pressures and motives that are behind decisions in this Act:

- Hathorne and Danforth believe that any turning back will undermine the whole legal structure.

- Reverend Hale is driven by guilt because he has signed death warrants.

- Parris is frightened for his own life.

- Elizabeth wants to prove to her husband that she trusts and respects him.

- Proctor wants to live and look after his family, but he chooses to die and keep his good name.

? DID YOU KNOW

Arthur Miller was fined for refusing to give names of people who had attended a communist meeting when he was questioned at the Un-American Activities Hearings.

CHECKPOINT 22

How has Hale changed from his behaviour in Act One?

Page 117: Echoes down the corridor

After the events of this play, Miller tells us that:

❶ Parris was voted out of office and never heard of again.

❷ Abigail is said to have turned up as a prostitute in Boston.

❸ Twenty years later, compensation was awarded to surviving victims and families of the dead.

❹ Some of the accusers still refused to admit they had been wrong.

❺ Some farms belonging to the victims remained unoccupied for up to one hundred years.

GRADE BOOSTER

Remember that Miller was making a political point with *The Crucible* as well as providing entertainment. To get the best grades you should be able to see beyond the simple story.

WHY IS THIS SECTION IMPORTANT?

A This **afterword** helps to make the drama feel authentic.

B As in a true crime story, we are told about the **consequences** of people's actions.

C This helps to remind us that the play was based on **real events** and real people.

D We are more inclined to **think** about the **ideas** in the play and relate them to our own times.

Progress and revision check

REVISION ACTIVITY

❶ What had Abigail and the girls been doing in the woods when Reverend Parris saw them? (Write your answers below)

....

❷ Why is John Proctor reluctant to get involved in the trials? What is his guilty secret?

....

❸ Why does Reverend Hale visit the Proctors?

....

❹ What does Mary Warren bring home from the court for Elizabeth?

....

❺ What is Rebecca Nurse accused of?

....

❻ Why does John Proctor tear up his signed confession?

....

REVISION ACTIVITY

On a piece of paper write down answers to these questions:

● Why are some people ready to believe the girls' accusations of witchcraft?

Start: *Many people truly believed in the Devil and witches but other reasons included …*

● What choices did the accused have and how did the court deal with those who tried to defend them?

Start: *People who were accused could either plead …*

GRADE BOOSTER ★

Answer this longer, practice question about the plot/action of the play:

Q: How do the events of the play hold the interest of the audience? Think about:

● John Proctor's guilty secret, which we are aware of but most of the other characters are not.
● Abigail's plot against Elizabeth.
● The sudden arrest of Elizabeth.
● How Reverend Hale changes his opinion of the trials.
● How John Proctor decides his own fate.

For a C grade: Convey your ideas clearly and appropriately (you could use the words from the question to guide your answer) and refer to details from the text (use specific examples).

For an A grade: Make sure you comment on the ways in which dramatic tension is created through fear, superstition and confusion and how the audience is encouraged to care about the outcome of the story and the fates of the central characters. Develop your ideas and back them up by using key details from the text.

John Proctor

WHO IS JOHN PROCTOR?

John Proctor is an honest, independent and plain-speaking farmer. He is married to Elizabeth. Although some people criticise his religious commitment, he is generally respected in Salem. However, he has a guilty secret. He has committed adultery with Abigail when she was his servant.

WHAT DOES JOHN PROCTOR DO IN THE PLAY?

- Proctor speaks his mind and stands up to Reverend Parris.

- He is scornful about the witchcraft hysteria but is cautious in his opposition to the trials at first.

- He persuades Mary Warren to tell the truth in court.

- As a last resort, he confesses to his adultery in order to expose Abigail, but he is defeated by Elizabeth's well-intentioned lie and by Abigail's power over the girls.

- In prison he confesses to witchcraft so that he can live and look after his family, but he will not name others.

- Finally, he refuses to sign a confession and decides to die rather than lose his good name.

HOW IS JOHN PROCTOR DESCRIBED AND WHAT DOES IT MEAN?

Quotation	Means?
'a sharp and biting way with hypocrites' (p. 16)	Miller's note here suggests why Proctor could easily make enemies in Salem.
'powerful of body, even-tempered and not easily led' (p. 16)	This describes Proctor's strength and independence.
'He is a sinner' (p. 16)	We are told that Proctor is burdened by a heavy sense of guilt.
'respected and even feared in Salem' (p. 16)	This again suggests his position in the community.

GRADE BOOSTER

Is John Proctor a thoroughly sympathetic character? Try drawing a graph to show how he goes up (or down) in your estimation during the play.

Quotation	Means?
'it is a man in his prime we see, with a quiet confidence and an unexpressed, hidden force.' (p. 16)	Proctor is an impressive presence in the room.
'I do not think I saw you at Sabbath meeting since snow flew.' (p. 23)	He is subject to criticism for his poor attendance at church.
'I do not judge you. The magistrate sits in your heart that judges you.' (p. 45)	Elizabeth knows that her husband is tortured by guilt for his adultery.
'... this man is mischief.' (p. 71)	Parris knows that Proctor is a formidable opponent when he comes to court and tries to discredit him.
'From the beginning this man has struck me true.' (p. 91)	Reverend Hale has always been impressed by Proctor and believes he is an honest man.
'Whatever you will do, it is a good man does it ... I never knew such goodness in the world.' (p. 109–10)	Elizabeth shows her belief in her husband and his decision.

KEY CONNECTION

Daniel Day-Lewis played the role of John Proctor in the 1996 film of the play.

EXAMINER'S TIP: WRITING ABOUT JOHN PROCTOR 🔓

John Proctor is the central character in Miller's play and suffers the trials and confusion of an ordinary reasonable man caught up in dangerous and unreasonable times. There is a strong connection here between his situation and that experienced by Arthur Miller in the anti-Communist hearings he was called before.

Proctor represents common sense and decency. He is not perfect, however, and is very aware of his own faults. Proctor is his own harshest judge. He believes strongly in telling the truth but he is tortured by the knowledge that he is living a lie.

He is a reluctant leader among those who oppose Parris and the Putnams. At first he only wants to save his wife, but later he comes to realise how important his good name is to him. Throughout the play Proctor is under great pressure when dealing with the struggle inside him between truth and reputation.

Elizabeth Proctor

WHO IS ELIZABETH PROCTOR?

Elizabeth is the wife of John Proctor. We hear she is a religious woman but rather cold. She has tried to forgive her husband but has been deeply hurt by his behaviour. She is, however, extremely loyal to John.

WHAT DOES ELIZABETH PROCTOR DO IN THE PLAY?

- Elizabeth says she does not judge her husband but she is unhappy when he is reluctant to go to court to confront Abigail and the girls.

- She suspects that Abigail still has some hold over him.

- She is accused of witchcraft and arrested, but she is not hanged immediately as she is found to be pregnant.

- In court she denies Proctor's adultery. She tells this lie to protect her husband's good name but does not realise that he has already made a public confession.

- Elizabeth will not confess to witchcraft and refuses to persuade her husband one way or the other.

- She confesses her own share of the blame for their marital problems.

- Elizabeth knows that Proctor must do what he believes to be right even if it means his execution.

HOW IS ELIZABETH DESCRIBED AND WHAT DOES IT MEAN?

Quotation	Means?
'She is a cold snivelling woman' (p. 19)	Abigail hates Elizabeth and wishes to replace her.
'Oh, Elizabeth, your justice would freeze beer!' (p. 46)	John Proctor feels that Elizabeth has not forgiven him.
'I am a covenanted Christian woman.' (p. 55)	Elizabeth is proud and confident of her religious standing.
'That woman will never lie, Mr Danforth' (p. 74)	Proctor is proud of his wife's honesty.

> **KEY QUOTE**
>
> Elizabeth: 'She [Mary] frightened all my strength away.' (p. 43)

Quotation	Means?
'My wife is innocent, except she knew a whore when she saw one!' (p. 89)	Proctor suggests that Elizabeth is only in court because she threw Abigail out of her house.
'In her life, sir, she have never lied.' (p. 89)	Proctor is confident that Elizabeth will support the truth of his confession.

EXAMINER'S TIP: WRITING ABOUT ELIZABETH PROCTOR

We first hear about Elizabeth from her enemy and rival, Abigail: 'She is a cold snivelling woman' (p. 19). When we see John Proctor and Elizabeth together, she is obviously still deeply hurt by his adultery and not altogether sure of his loyalty towards her. This comes across as coldness, and we feel some sympathy for Proctor as we have seen him strongly spurn Abigail's advances.

Elizabeth is a devout Christian and proud of it, which may add to our impression of her primness and sense of moral superiority.

She is, however, mainly a victim through no fault of her own. She makes the tragic mistake of lying in court to protect her husband's good name.

Although she is spared execution because of her pregnancy, Elizabeth refuses to persuade Proctor to save his own life by confessing to witchcraft. This shows her strength and her belief in her husband: 'He have his goodness now. God forbid I take it from him!' (p. 116).

EXAMINER'S TIP

Remember that as well as being well-drawn portraits, characters often have specific roles to play and purposes to serve in the drama.

Reverend John Hale

WHO IS REVEREND JOHN HALE?

Hale is a respected religious scholar who arrives in Salem to give advice on the witchcraft problem. He means well but is proved to be weak. He turns against the court but is unable to halt the executions.

WHAT DOES JOHN HALE DO IN THE PLAY?

- Hale comes to Salem as an expert in religious matters in answer to a request from Reverend Parris.

- He exhorts Tituba and the girls to confess and to denounce others to save themselves.

- When the girls start naming people as witches, he is delighted with his success: 'Glory to God! It is broken, they are free!' (p. 39).

- When he begins to lose confidence in the trials, he visits people in the parish to find out for himself what they are like.

- He arrives at the Proctors' house in Act Two and questions them about their religious practices and beliefs.

- Surprised by the arrest of Elizabeth, he tries to reassure John Proctor and promises to speak up for Elizabeth in court.

- Hale is troubled by the death warrants he has signed and finally he storms out of court, crying out, 'I denounce these proceedings!' (p. 96).

- In Act Four, Hale tries to undo some of the harm he has helped to bring about.

- He asks Danforth to pardon the condemned people.

- He begs those under sentence of death to confess to witchcraft and so save their lives. Unlike the prisoners, he is prepared to give up his principles to salve his guilty conscience.

GRADE BOOSTER

Consider how Hale's doubts about the witch-hunt and his response to Proctor's information about the girls raise the dramatic tension by giving us hope that Abigail and her friends will be exposed as liars.

HOW IS REVEREND JOHN HALE DESCRIBED AND WHAT DOES IT MEAN?

Quotation	Means?
'nearing forty, a tight-skinned, eager-eyed intellectual.' (p. 26)	Hale is described as physically fit and mentally alert.
'he felt the pride of the specialist' (p. 26)	He believes he has brought the answers to all their questions.

Quotation	Means?
'Hale feels himself allied with the best minds of Europe' (p. 30)	Hale is very proud that he is in touch with the latest religious theories.
'His goal, is light, goodness and its preservation' (p. 30)	In his view, he comes with the highest motives.
'He is different now – drawn a little, and there is a quality of deference, even of guilt, about his manner now.' (p. 52)	There are signs in his appearance and in his personality that the trials are beginning to have a wearing effect on him.
'You are a coward! Though you be ordained in God's own tears, you are a coward now!' (p. 64)	John Proctor denounces Hale's weak response to the arrests of Rebecca Nurse and Elizabeth.
'Mr Hale, believe me; for a man of such terrible learning you are most bewildered – ' (p. 80)	Danforth thinks that Hale is wasting his time defending the accused people as there is no way to prove their innocence.
'He is steeped in sorrow, exhausted, and more direct than he ever was.' (p. 103)	Hale is practically a broken man.
'... where I turned the eye of my great faith, blood flowed up.' (p. 106)	He believes that his religious expertise has brought nothing but death to Salem.

★ **GRADE BOOSTER**

Don't forget Arthur Miller's long introduction to Hale on pp. 26–30 and the extra historical detail the playwright provides here.

EXAMINER'S TIP: WRITING ABOUT REVEREND JOHN HALE 🔓

It is important to consider the reversal in the moral position of Reverend Hale. At the beginning of the play, he is the confident religious expert, respected and admired. He has come to Salem to solve the town's problems. He has brought his books with him and seems to have immediate success. By the end he is a broken man, rejected and scorned by the Proctors. 'I think that be the Devil's argument' (p. 106), says Elizabeth, when he tries to persuade her that her husband should lie to save his own life. It is John Proctor who occupies the moral high ground at the end of the play.

Hale is despised by the court and in despair about where his religious expertise has brought him: 'what I touched with my bright confidence, it died' (p. 106). We may feel some sympathy for Hale as he has come to doubt the girls and to believe in the innocence of the accused, but we cannot help feeling that he is largely driven by his guilt for signing death warrants.

Abigail Williams

WHO IS ABIGAIL WILLIAMS?

Abigail Williams is Reverend Parris's niece. She was a servant of the Proctors but was dismissed by Elizabeth for having an affair with John. She is the leader of the girls involved in the trials and uses her power to secure Elizabeth's conviction for witchcraft as she hopes to replace her as John's wife.

WHAT DOES ABIGAIL DO IN THE PLAY?

- Abigail dominates the other girls as they cry witchcraft to escape punishment for their escapades in the forest.

- She tries to persuade John Proctor to restart their affair.

- Abigail implicates Elizabeth by suggesting that the 'poppet' with a needle stuck in it is Elizabeth's, and a form of witchcraft against her.

- When Mary Warren is exposing their fraud, Abigail distracts the court and destroys Mary's confidence by pretending to feel a cold wind and see a spirit in the form of a yellow bird.

- In Act Four, we hear that Abigail has stolen her uncle's money and has run away with Mercy Lewis.

HOW IS ABIGAIL DESCRIBED AND WHAT DOES IT MEAN?

Quotation	Means?
'a strikingly beautiful girl' (p. 6)	We can see why John Proctor has been physically attracted to her.
'an endless capacity for dissembling' (p. 6)	We are warned about her dishonesty.
'You'll be clapped in the stocks before you're twenty.' (p. 17)	Proctor is half joking here about her recklessness. He does not realise how far she will go.
'where she walks the crowd will part like the sea for Israel.' (p. 43)	Abigail is now the most important witness in the witchcraft trials. She inspires fear.

Quotation	Means?
'She wants me dead, John, you know it!' (p. 50)	Elizabeth understands Abigail's plan to marry Proctor.
'She has an arrow in you yet, John Proctor, and you know it well!' (p. 52)	Elizabeth believes that Abigail still holds some attraction for her husband.
'She thinks to dance with me on my wife's grave!' (p. 89)	Proctor denounces Abigail in court for plotting against his wife.
'This girl has always struck me false!' (p. 91)	Reverend Hale confesses that he has always had doubts about Abigail.
'You are pulling Heaven down and raising up a whore!' (p. 96)	This is Proctor's final condemnation of the court for believing in Abigail.

EXAMINER'S TIP: WRITING ABOUT ABIGAIL WILLIAMS

Abigail is important because she is the cause of John Proctor's guilt and because she has such influence over the other girls. She has a very powerful personality and inspires fear in the population of Salem once the trials begin. She is able to destroy Proctor's plan of defence even at the point when things are going against her. She does this by her ability to inspire hysteria in the weaker girls, even overpowering Mary Warren who has come to give evidence against her.

Abigail's cunning and total lack of morals is underlined by the way she runs off with her uncle's money when things are becoming dangerous for her in Salem.

Her behaviour could be described as purely evil, and yet in some ways she has been a victim, a young orphan seduced and then rejected by her employer, John Proctor.

EXAMINER'S TIP

If you can, try to see the different sides to each character. Miller is known for showing many dimensions to his characters.

Mary Warren

WHO IS MARY WARREN?

Mary Warren is the timid young servant of John and Elizabeth Proctor. She has been dancing in the woods with Abigail and the others, and becomes involved as a witness in the trials.

WHAT DOES MARY WARREN DO IN THE PLAY?

- Mary attends the witchcraft trials and denounces people for witchcraft.

- She brings a 'poppet' to the Proctors' house. This is part of Abigail's plot against Elizabeth.

- John Proctor persuades her to go to court to tell the truth, but Abigail is too strong for her and she turns against Proctor.

GRADE BOOSTER

Would the outcome of the play be different, do you think, if Mary had stood up to Abigail?

HOW IS MARY WARREN DESCRIBED AND WHAT DOES IT MEAN?

Quotation	Means?
'a subservient, naive, lonely girl.' (p. 14)	Mary is easily led and easily impressed by Abigail.
'It is a mouse no more. I forbid her to go, and she raises up her chin like the daughter of a prince ...' (p. 43)	The attention Mary is given at the court makes her bold enough to defy Elizabeth.
'She has been strivin' with her soul all week, your Honour; she comes now to tell the truth of this to you.' (p. 70)	Mary has been persuaded to own up to lying.

EXAMINER'S TIP: WRITING ABOUT MARY WARREN

Mary is a shy girl and obviously timid. However, she provides humour on occasions when she tries to be dignified, for example refusing to go to bed, then going when told she may stay (pp. 49–50).

Reverend Parris

WHO IS REVEREND PARRIS?

Reverend Parris is the unpopular minister of the parish. He is worried about his reputation when he has seen his daughter Betty and his niece Abigail dancing in the woods.

WHAT DOES REVEREND PARRIS DO IN THE PLAY?

- Parris has sent for Reverend Hale, the witchcraft expert, because his daughter Betty will not wake up.

- He quarrels with his parishioners about his income and ownership of church property.

- Parris supports the witchcraft trials but becomes frightened when there is talk of civil unrest and rebellion as a consequence.

 **GRADE BOOSTER**

Reverend Parris and Reverend Hale both have important roles to play. Make a list of their similarities and differences.

HOW IS REVEREND PARRIS DESCRIBED AND WHAT DOES IT MEAN?

Quotation	Means?
'I have trouble enough without I come five mile to hear him preach only hellfire and bloody damnation.' (p. 23)	John Proctor speaks for those in the parish who dislike Parris's negative preaching.
'... the first minister ever did demand the deed to this house.' (p. 24)	Parris is seen to be unusually greedy for a minister.
'Mr Parris, you are a brainless man!' (p. 101)	Governor Danforth has nothing but contempt for Parris and shows no sympathy when he has been robbed by Abigail.

EXAMINER'S TIP: WRITING ABOUT REVEREND PARRIS

Parris demonstrates how difficult it is for an official in a position of authority to hide hypocrisy, greed and cowardice. We quickly realise we have to look to other characters for moral courage and decency.

The Putnams

Thomas Putnam is a wealthy farmer who is greedy for more land. His wife Ann is a bitter woman who has lost seven children at birth and is looking for someone or something to blame. In the play:

- The Putnams take Reverend Parris's side in the parish.
- Ann Putnam is jealous of Rebecca Nurse, who has a large family and is charged with murdering Ann's children.
- Thomas is accused by Giles Corey of encouraging his daughter to denounce people so that he can buy their land cheaply.

HOW ARE THE PUTNAMS DESCRIBED AND WHAT DOES IT MEAN?

Quotation	Means?
'a man with many grievances' (p. 11)	Thomas is suspicious and resentful.
'a death-ridden woman, haunted by dreams.' (p. 9)	The loss of so many children has deeply affected Ann Putnam's mind.
'This man is killing his neighbours for that land!' (p. 77)	In court, Giles Corey accuses Thomas of conspiracy to murder.

The Nurses

Rebecca Nurse is well known for her good works and Christian charity. Francis is her faithful husband.

- At the beginning of the play, it is Rebecca who calms Betty by her mere presence.
- She tries to discourage Reverend Hale from taking drastic action and suggests that 'good prayer' (p. 22) may be the best answer.
- Francis comes with Giles Corey to John Proctor's house when their wives have been arrested.
- In court, he joins with Proctor and Giles in the defence of their wives.

HOW ARE THE NURSES DESCRIBED AND WHAT DOES IT MEAN?

Quotation	Means?
'one of those men for whom both sides of the argument had to have respect.' (p. 20)	Francis has a reputation as fair, honest and unbiased.
'My wife is the very brick and mortar of the church' (p. 58)	Francis knows that his wife helps to hold the religious community together.
'if Rebecca Nurse be tainted, then nothing's left to stop the whole green world from burning.' (p. 58)	Even Hale realises that Rebecca is the last person one would suspect of witchcraft.

GRADE BOOSTER

The Putnams represent the underlying jealousies and quarrels among the population which feed the accusations of witchcraft. Make sure you can write about how this becomes a way of settling old scores in Salem.

EXAMINER'S TIP

You could write about how Rebecca's conviction demonstrates the extreme extent of the witchcraft hysteria. The Nurses represent the most decent and religious elements of the community. There seems to be no hope that anyone can prove their innocence after this.

Tituba and minor characters

TITUBA

Tituba is the slave Reverend Parris has brought from Barbados. She is an exotic figure in the community. The girls encouraged her to carry out voodoo rituals in the woods. 'You beg *me* to conjure!' (p. 36), she shouts, when Abigail tries to blame her. Even Ann Putnam has tried to enlist her help to contact her dead children. She is terrified and will confess to anything. In jail, she fantasises about flying to Barbados with the Devil.

GILES COREY

Giles Corey is an argumentative old farmer who has had legal disputes with many of his neighbours. When his wife is arrested, he goes to court with John Proctor and Francis Nurse. We hear that he keeps silent when he is charged rather than deny witchcraft; otherwise, his land would be confiscated.

Giles provides some humour in the play when arguing with his neighbours and with Danforth in the court, but he dies a hero, calling for more weight as he is pressed to death with stones.

BETTY

Betty is Parris's ten-year-old daughter. Her strange illness triggers the fears of witchcraft in Salem. She is under Abigail's influence and takes part in the court proceedings.

MERCY LEWIS AND SUSANNA WALCOTT

Mercy Lewis is the Putnams' servant. She is a sly and vindictive girl who denounces people and is in court with the others. After the trials, we hear that she has run away with Abigail. Susanna is a young, nervous and frightened member of Abigail's group.

JUDGE HATHORNE

Hathorne is a cold, unbending judge who believes that anyone protesting against the sentences must be in league with the accused and guilty of attacking the court.

DEPUTY-GOVERNOR DANFORTH

Danforth is more reasonable than Hathorne and is prepared to listen to new evidence such as Mary Warren's confession of having lied. However, he is firm in his defence of the court: 'a person is either with this court or ... against it' (p. 76).

MARSHAL HERRICK

Herrick is an officer of the court. He is a kindly man and is obviously unhappy about arresting people like Elizabeth Proctor and keeping them in jail: 'In God's name, John, I cannot help myself. I must chain them all' (p. 64).

KEY QUOTE

Elizabeth: 'Aye. It were a fearsome man, Giles Corey.' (p. 108)

EXAMINER'S TIP

Don't forget that even minor characters have roles to play:

- Ezekiel Cheever is Clerk of the Court and serves the warrant on Elizabeth Proctor. He is a petty and pompous man without humour.
- Sarah Good is a poor confused old woman who confesses to witchcraft and shares a cell with Tituba.

Progress and revision check

Revision activity

❶ How is John Proctor described? (Write your answers below)

....

❷ Describe the relationship between Proctor and his wife Elizabeth in Act Two. How does it change by the end of the play?

....

❸ Why do the girls accuse people of witchcraft? What particular motive does Abigail have?

....

❹ What motivates Ann and Thomas Putnam to denounce their neighbours?

....

❺ Why is Mary Warren defeated by Abigail when she confesses to lying in court?

....

❻ Why does John Proctor tear up his confession and choose to hang?

....

Revision activity

On a piece of paper write down answers to these questions:

● What part does Reverend John Hale play in the events?
  Start: *Reverend Hale is important because ...*

● How do Rebecca and Francis Nurse and Giles Corey contribute to the drama?
  Start: *The Nurses and Giles Corey add to the drama because they are ...*

GRADE BOOSTER ★

Examine the progress of John Proctor in the play and how he deals with the problems he faces. Think about:

● Proctor's feelings towards Abigail

● his relationship with Elizabeth

● his response to the witchcraft trials, before and after Elizabeth's arrest

● his behaviour in prison in Act Four.

For a C grade: Check that you have mentioned the relevant facts and support your comments with details from the text. If you use direct quotations, explain what they mean.

For an A grade: Examine the ideas behind the spoken words. Look at the ways in which character is revealed through language. Support your comments by reference to the text. Think about your own response to the character and also why the author chose to present him in this way. You will find ideas to discuss by referring to Arthur Miller's notes.

Key contexts

THE AUTHOR

Arthur Miller was born in New York on 17 October 1915 and was brought up in the Brooklyn area of that city. His father was a clothing manufacturer whose small business collapsed in the financial depression of the 1930s, a period when many people like him went bankrupt.

After leaving school Miller worked for two years in a car parts warehouse to make enough money to pay for higher education. At the University of Michigan he won an award for his first play, a comedy, *The Grass Still Grows*. After leaving college Miller had some success with radio dramas and in 1944 his play *The Man Who Had All The Luck* was performed on Broadway. This did not make much money but it won him New York's Theatre Guild Award.

Miller's first real success was *All My Sons*, about a father who is forced to realise the dangerous moral compromises he has made in chasing the American Dream of wealth in wartime. But his biggest theatrical hit and his most highly acclaimed work was *Death of a Salesman* (1949), which won him, among other awards, the Pulitzer Prize.

The Crucible won awards in 1953 but was not an immediate commercial success. Arthur Miller continued to be a major dramatist, however, with *A View from the Bridge* (1955) and *After the Fall* (1964) following on. He was always ready to deal with difficult and controversial issues and tried to make his audiences consider both unpleasant and uplifting aspects of human behaviour.

WITCHCRAFT

For many hundreds of years throughout Europe there was a belief in witchcraft. At times this belief developed into hysterical fear, leading to campaigns of persecution against suspected witches.

Some of the accused, who were mainly women, may have had a knowledge of herbal medicine or other folk remedies. Superstitious people would assume that they had magical powers or were in league with the Devil. In a time of fear it would be easy to accuse someone you did not like and very difficult for the accused to prove their innocence.

Some scholars became experts in witchcraft and believed that they knew how to identify witches. It was thought that witches were agents of the Devil and that they could change their shape. Many thousands of people accused of being witches were tortured and executed throughout the Middle Ages and up to the seventeenth century. The authorities used the text from Exodus 22:18 to justify these killings: 'Thou shalt not suffer a witch to live.'

? DID YOU KNOW

Two of Arthur Miller's plays, *Death of a Salesman* and *A View from the Bridge*, are set in Brooklyn, where Miller grew up.

? DID YOU KNOW

The salesman Willie Loman, the central character of *Death of a Salesman*, is destroyed by his dependence on the false values of the business world to which he has devoted his life. He is perhaps Miller's best-known character.

KEY CONNECTION

James I wrote a book on witchcraft in 1597, before he was King of England.

KEY CONNECTION

The Scarlet Letter by the American writer Nathaniel Hawthorne, published in 1850, is set against a background not dissimilar to that of *The Crucible* – seventeenth-century Puritan Massachusetts.

KEY CONNECTION

In 1996 Arthur Miller completed a screenplay for a film of *The Crucible*, which was released in 1997 starring Daniel Day-Lewis and Winona Ryder. Try watching the film and comparing it to the play.

SALEM, MASSACHUSETTS

This belief in witchcraft persisted among the English colonists who left Europe for America. In 1692 there was an outbreak of accusations of witchcraft in Salem, Massachusetts. The colonists there were Puritans who strictly followed a particular form of Protestant Christianity. They felt surrounded by ungodly people and associated the forest with savages and with evil.

Two young girls had been taking part in magic ceremonies. Ministers, doctors and magistrates were called in and soon accusations multiplied. Before the panic burned itself out, twenty people had been executed (one man was pressed to death by stones) and about two hundred had been accused. Later some of the witnesses and judges who had been involved publicly regretted what had happened.

THE COLD WAR

In modern times the term 'witch-hunt' has come to mean the searching out and persecution of religious or political dissidents – that is, people who have views different from those of the majority and who may be considered a threat to the community.

After the Second World War, relations between the United States of America and the Soviet Union deteriorated and there followed a period known as the Cold War. Many people in the United States feared that the Russians were aiming to take over the world. This led to a fear of Communism in the United States.

EXAMINER'S TIP: WRITING ABOUT MCCARTHYISM AND *THE CRUCIBLE*

American Senator Joe McCarthy organised a twentieth-century version of witch-hunting. In the early 1950s he exploited US fears about Communism and managed to create a national campaign against Communists. *The Crucible* was first produced in 1953. This was when McCarthy's anti-Communist campaign was at its height, and there are obvious parallels in the play: unsupported accusations; people encouraged to denounce their friends and acquaintances; a spiral of fear and suspicion. People who were arrested in the United States included well-respected writers and film-makers. Arthur Miller himself was called in front of the **Un-American Activities Committee** in 1956. Miller refused to give the names of friends who might have been interested in Communism, and he was fined for contempt of Congress. Miller himself tended to play this down.

Key themes

PURIFICATION

A crucible is a container in which metals and other materials are heated so as to separate the pure metals from waste and impurities. The crucible in the title is a **metaphor** for the town of Salem and the period of the witch-hunt hysteria. In this 'fire', some victims survive the temptations and fears and emerge as better and stronger people.

TYRANNY

The Crucible shows a group of people reacting within a state of tyranny – in this case tyranny exerted by a small group, who manipulate a situation for their own purposes and choose to misinterpret events for their own ends. Finally, the situation and the events develop their own momentum and veer out of control.

REVISION ACTIVITY

Here are some key incidents related to the **theme** of tyranny. Explain why each one is important.

- Parris sends for Reverend Hale.
- Abigail hits Betty across the face: 'Shut it! Now shut it!' (p. 15).
- The court arrests many people on the word of the girls alone (Act Two).
- Danforth announces, 'No uncorrupted man may fear this court' (p. 79).
- Danforth forces Proctor into an impossible situation in Act Four.

BIGOTRY

Throughout the events in Salem, we see the effects of religious zeal, fear of heresy, intolerance and superstition. Reverend Hale is so proud of his knowledge of witchcraft that he is quick to accept the girls' confessions as proof of this skill. Others are more than willing to accept supernatural reasons or 'unnatural causes' (p. 7) for their problems. There is so much insecurity in the young colony that anyone who questions the authorities, either religious or state, is seen to be launching an attack on the whole foundation of society.

CONFLICT

The conflict between the security of the community and 'individual freedom' (p. 5) is one theme that runs through the play. Salem was a community that felt under siege, threatened by the dangers of the wilderness, the possible corrupting influences of other Christian sects, and a genuine fear of the Devil. The play has obvious parallels with the McCarthy investigations, which were proceeding when it was first produced. *The Crucible* has been seen by some as a simple **allegory** of the abuse of state power by those who persecuted and denounced people who were thought to be undermining the American way of life. Just as in Salem, those who opposed McCarthy's investigations were treated as enemies of the state.

INTEGRITY

Honesty and personal integrity are important themes. The most admirable characters who retain their dignity are those who will not tell lies. Rebecca Nurse and Elizabeth Proctor are shining examples: both insist on the truth, regardless of the consequences for themselves. John Proctor is finally at peace with himself when he decides to die rather than give up his good name. He is purified in the 'crucible' of the stresses and temptations he is subjected to. On the other hand, Reverend Hale (who at the end begs Proctor to lie, admit to witchcraft and save his life) is miserable, mentally tortured and morally ruined.

KEY CONNECTION

Arthur Koestler's *Darkness at Noon*, published in 1940, is set in an unnamed country, but one that people have identified as 1930s Russia, under Stalin's cruel regime. A revolutionary is encouraged to confess to crimes he did not commit, for the good of the state.

KEY CONNECTION

For some extra background, look at two novels that deal with seventeenth-century witch-hunts, this time in Lancashire: *The Lancashire Witches* by William Harrison Ainsworth (1848; Grafton Books, 1988) and *Mist over Pendle* by Robert Neill (Arrow, 1992).

LOYALTY

Loyalty is a **theme** that is illustrated in the behaviour of John Proctor towards his friends. He is tempted to withdraw his charges against Abigail and her group when he is told that his wife is pregnant and is not in immediate danger of hanging, but he goes ahead to support his friends whose wives have also been accused. Elizabeth, although she has been badly hurt by her husband's affair with Abigail, is too loyal to shame him in court and denies knowledge of it. **Ironically**, her loyalty destroys John's case against Abigail.

REVISION ACTIVITY

Here are some key incidents related to the theme of loyalty. Explain why each one is important.

- Abigail wants Proctor to betray his wife and to be loyal to her instead.

- Elizabeth remains loyal to Proctor.

- Mary Warren is too weak to show loyalty to the family that has taken her in.

- Hale thinks he is being loyal to the court.

COURAGE

We are shown courage in the behaviour of the accused, particularly Rebecca Nurse. As she goes to be hanged, she tells John Proctor to 'fear nothing!' (p. 116) as another judgement awaits them. Proctor tells his wife to defy the authorities and to show them no tears. We hear of Giles Corey's stubborn courage in refusing to answer the charges so that his sons may inherit his farm. His last defiant words, as he was being crushed to death, were 'More weight' (p. 108).

ENVY

Envy and resentment are demonstrated in the Putnams' quarrels over land and Ann Putnam's bitter feelings towards Rebecca Nurse and her healthy family. These feelings are converted to self-serving accusations of witchcraft. Abigail is envious of Elizabeth's position as Proctor's wife and it is possible that she believes that she can take her place once Elizabeth is out of the way.

REVISION ACTIVITY

Here are some key incidents related to the theme of envy. Explain why each one is important.

- Putnam wants other people's land.

- Abigail is envious of Elizabeth Proctor.

- Giles Corey has had court cases against some of his neighbours.

Progress and revision check

REVISION ACTIVITY

❶ What are the residents of Salem afraid of? (Write your answers below)

....

❷ What is the name of the senator who organised 'witch-hunts' in America in the 1950s?

....

❸ Who is the most loyal character in the play?

....

❹ Why do the Putnams want revenge on Rebecca Nurse?

....

❺ What is a crucible?

....

REVISION ACTIVITY

On a piece of paper write down answers to these questions:

● What different types of conflict are there in the play?

Start: *The most important type of conflict in the play is between …*

● Why is Abigail a tyrannical character?

Start: *Abigail is a tyrannical character because …*

GRADE BOOSTER

Answer this longer, practice question about the themes in the play:

Examine the role of integrity in *The Crucible*. Think about:

● the behaviour of Rebecca Nurse and Elizabeth Proctor

● the contrast with the behaviour of Abigail, Parris and the Putnams

● the atmosphere of the play

● how the theme develops.

For a C grade: Check that you have mentioned the relevant facts and support your comments with details from the text. If you use direct quotations, explain what they mean.

For an A grade: Examine the context behind the play. Look at the ways in which the theme is revealed through language and character interaction. Support your comments by reference to the text. Think about your own response to the question and the overall message that Arthur Miller wanted to convey.

Language

Here are some useful terms to know when writing about *The Crucible*, what they mean and how they appear in the play.

EXAMINER'S TIP

Don't only include what you think the examiner wants you to say. Success is likely to follow when you give a personal response!

Literary term	Means?	Example
allegory	A story that can be seen to have two different and parallel meanings, rather like a fable or parable	*The Crucible* can be read as an allegory of the anti-Communist investigations in the United States in the 1950s.
atmosphere	A mood or feeling created by the language, action or setting	An atmosphere of suspicion and claustrophobia is created by the tightly controlled community and power struggles within it.
colloquial	Everyday speech that is often particular to a certain place or region	Miller uses colloquial language such as 'it rebels my stomach' to give richness to everyday ideas.
inversion/ inverted	A departure from normal word order	In *The Crucible* **inversion** is used to represent an older form of English: 'I know not what I have said', 'I like not the sound of it'.
irony/ironic	Using words to convey the opposite of their literal meaning, a deliberate contrast between apparent and intended meaning; also a mismatch between what might be expected and what actually occurs	Proctor's comment that Hale is known to be a 'sensible man' is ironic in that Hale is partly responsible for the hysteria and madness that follows his investigations.
metaphor	A description of one thing in terms of something else	Proctor uses this ominous metaphor to describe his fate: 'I have made a bell of my honour! I have rung the doom of my good name.'
simile	A direct comparison of one thing with another, using 'like', 'as' or 'as if'	Parris doesn't want to be 'put out like the cat' by the villagers when they grow tired of him.

THE LANGUAGE CHARACTERS SPEAK

The language spoken by the characters in the play is intended to give us the feeling of a society that is quite different from ours. When he was researching the play, Miller was intrigued by the language of the court records and adapted some of it for his dialogue. He does not use the exact form of English that the people of Salem would have recognised as this might prove too difficult for a modern audience to understand. Instead, Miller gives us a flavour of the language spoken in seventeenth-century America.

Miller uses double negatives and **inverted** sentence structures in his version of this language. John Proctor says, 'I never said no such thing' (p. 25); Giles Corey tells Danforth, 'I will not give you no name' (p. 78). In Act Four, Danforth tells Elizabeth 'we come not for your life' (p. 105) when the modern version would be 'we do not come for your life', while 'What think you, Mr Parris?' (p. 104) would be 'What do you think?'. In his autobiography *Timebends*, Miller said of the language:

> I came to love its feel, like hard burnished wood. Without planning to, I even elaborated a few of the grammatical forms myself, the double negatives especially, which occurred in the trial record much less frequently than they would in the play.

Some words are used in a way that we would not use them now. Giles Corey, complaining about his wife's reading habits, says, 'It discomforts me!' (p. 33), using 'discomfort' as a verb, whereas we would say, 'It makes me uncomfortable.' John Proctor expresses amazement that Mr Hale would 'suspicion' his wife (p. 57). Modern usage would be 'suspect'.

EXAMINER'S TIP: WRITING ABOUT THE INFLUENCE OF LATIN

For centuries, Latin had been used by the church in order to keep the Bible from ordinary people. As they were not able to read it for themselves, knowledge was kept in the hands of the church. The Puritans of Salem rebelled against the language itself but still spoke in a way that reflected the English of their home country, which was heavily influenced by Latin.

In Latin, the verb usually comes at the end of the sentence: for example, 'Up the stairs she climbed.' If you find that some of the word order in *The Crucible* is unusual, it is because we have now moved away from this way of constructing sentences.

★ **GRADE BOOSTER**

Note that in Act One, when Reverend Hale wants to drive out the Devil, he chants in Latin. Think about the effect this has: does it make him seem more powerful, and his words more mysterious?

CHRISTIANITY AND THE BIBLE

The rhythms and the **imagery** of the language of the play echo those of the Authorised or King James version of the Bible of 1611. The Puritans in England, forefathers of the Salem settlers, had requested a new translation of the Bible in English as part of their pressures for reform of the Church. It took seven years to complete and had a definite influence on style.

- The Authorised Version, used by Protestants for 350 years, was loved for the beauty and clarity of its English. It would have been familiar to the audiences of the 1950s and still is to many people today. It was only replaced by modern versions in around 1960.

- The first names of the characters and others mentioned are taken from the Bible. This was common practice in Christian communities. Some of the names that are not so commonly used today, such as Ezekiel, Isaac and Susanna, are from the Old Testament. Others, like John, Thomas, Martha and Elizabeth, can be found in the New Testament.

THE LANGUAGE OF RELIGION

A good deal of the language found in *The Crucible* has its origins in religion. Reverend Hale, when he describes his period of soul-searching before he tries to persuade John Proctor to save his life by confessing, says, 'I have gone this three months like our Lord into the wilderness' (p. 105). He is comparing his experience to that of Jesus when, according to St Matthew, he was 'led up of the Spirit into the wilderness to be tempted of the devil' (Matthew 4:1). In Act Two, speaking of Abigail, Elizabeth Proctor says, 'where she walks the crowd will part like the sea for Israel' (p. 43), which is a reference to the parting of the Red Sea in the book of Exodus when Moses led the Israelites in their escape from Egypt. When Danforth is asked to delay the executions, he replies, 'God have not empowered me like Joshua to stop this sun from rising' (p. 104), which refers to Joshua 10.

This is a powerful, dignified way of speaking which helps to create the impression of a different society, one that is rural and deeply religious. It is a deliberate and simple language, which is appropriate to the period in which the play is set without being too difficult for the modern audience.

Within this form of language some characters are made to be more eloquent than others. It is important that Abigail is an impressive speaker, whereas Mary Warren has to be more timid. It is not that the girls actually spoke exactly like this: it suits Miller's dramatic purpose to have the two girls speak differently from each other.

EXAMINER'S TIP: WRITING ABOUT LANGUAGE IN CONTEXT

Arthur Miller uses the rhythms and patterns of speech that would have been heard in Salem at the time of the original trials. You need to remember this when writing about the play. The characters are not speaking old English or even funny English. It is simply that the English we speak today has changed since the seventeenth century. If you need convincing of this, imagine how our speech might sound to people in four hundred years' time.

Structure

The Crucible is a tightly plotted play with plenty of drama, tension and contrast. Below is a summary of the important elements of each Act.

ACT ONE

The first Act establishes the conflicts that will develop through the play. Miller immediately presents the audience with the fear of witchcraft that is beginning to spread. The first Act also gives us the background to the conflicts within the small community of Salem. We see that there are disputes over land and dissatisfaction with the minister.

ACT TWO

The second Act shows us the uneasy relationship between John and Elizabeth Proctor. The tension is raised by the impending danger to Elizabeth and reaches a climax in the highly charged incident of her arrest. During most of this Act there are only two or three characters present and the drama is more intimate. The focus is on Proctor and Elizabeth, but Abigail's influence is felt throughout.

ACT THREE

The third Act takes place in the courtroom and presents us with the life-or-death struggle between superstition and reason. Hopes are raised and dashed. A crucial point in the drama is reached when Proctor confesses his adultery. We feel that this should finally destroy Abigail's credibility, but the tables are turned when Elizabeth's misplaced loyalty destroys his case. Mary Warren's attempt to recant is defeated by the force of Abigail's personality (and that of her followers), and she denounces John Proctor, who is arrested.

ACT FOUR: THE CLIMAX OF THE PLAY

The final Act allows us to see John Proctor grow into a noble and heroic character who chooses to die rather than deny himself and his good name. It is **ironic** that the once-proud Hale is reduced to the state of begging Proctor to lie to avoid being hanged. There is a dramatic twist when Proctor confesses and then recants. In this Act the relationship between Proctor and Elizabeth is seen to have grown stronger than ever.

REVISION ACTIVITY

The table on the next page shows how each of the four Acts takes place in one key location, and the role of the four main protagonists in each Act. As a revision exercise ask yourself the following questions and check your answers overleaf:

- Where does Act One take place?
- Where do we learn that Abigail has denounced Elizabeth?
- What happens to Elizabeth in the courtroom?
- In which Act does Proctor confess?

? DID YOU KNOW

The events in Salem actually took place in a number of different locations. Miller has reduced the number of locations to one per Act in order to make the drama function on stage.

	Act One	Act Two	Act Three	Act Four
	Reverend Parris's house	Proctor's house	Courtroom	Jail
John Proctor	Proctor quarrels with Parris. Rejects Abigail's advances	Proctor defends himself to Elizabeth and to Hale. Struggles against Elizabeth's arrest, gets Mary to recant	Proctor defends Elizabeth and neighbours' wives, confesses to adultery, encourages Mary to recant and is arrested	Proctor confesses, to live and look after his children, but tears up the confession and goes to die rather than besmirch his good name
Elizabeth	Elizabeth is spoken of as 'cold' by Abigail	Elizabeth is cool towards Proctor, satisfies Hale as to her character but is arrested on Abigail's word	We hear Elizabeth is pregnant and will not hang immediately. She is brought in to support Proctor's confession of adultery but she will not shame him publicly	Elizabeth allows Proctor to make up his own mind about confessing. She supports him and refuses to try to influence him when he chooses death
Reverend Hale	Reverend Hale arrives full of pride in his knowledge. He soon extracts 'confessions'	Hale has doubts about the witch-hunt and makes his own enquiries, visits the Proctors and is shocked by Elizabeth's arrest	Hale tries to intercede for the accused, finally denounces the court and leaves	Hale is a broken man, encouraging people to deny their faith to save their lives
Abigail	Abigail is in trouble through dancing in the woods and begins to denounce people. She shows desire for John Proctor and hatred for Elizabeth	We hear Abigail is the star witness in the witch trials. She has denounced Elizabeth	Abigail leads the girls in court. She defies Proctor and even Danforth. She defeats Mary Warren	We hear that Abigail has absconded with Reverend Parris's money

This table also helps to show the development of each of these characters, and the influence and impact they have across the play. Try making your own table for other characters such as Reverend Parris and Giles Corey.

Progress and revision check

REVISION ACTIVITY

❶ Which character speaks in Latin? (Write your answers below)

....

❷ Give an example of a metaphor from the play.

....

❸ Give an example of a simile from the play.

....

❹ Which Act takes place in the courtroom?

....

❺ In which Act does the climax of the play take place?

....

REVISION ACTIVITY

On a piece of paper write down answers to these questions:

● What type of language do the characters speak?

Start: *Arthur Miller uses the language of ...*

● How does Miller build tension throughout the play?

Start: *In Act One, Arthur Miller creates tension by ...*

GRADE BOOSTER

Answer this longer, practice question about the language of play:

Examine the role of religious language in *The Crucible*. Think about:

● the imagery and symbolism that is used

● the strict Puritan code of Salem

● the voices of different characters

● the atmosphere of fear and the importance of authority.

For a C grade: Check that you have found some powerful examples of religious language and say what effect these have on the play. Make sure you use direct quotations, and explain what they mean.

For an A grade: Show that you are aware of the different levels of meaning in the play. Look at the ways in which religious language sets the tone and influences events. Be prepared to say which factors you think are most important and why!

PART SIX: GRADE BOOSTER

Understanding the question

Questions in exams or controlled conditions often need **'decoding'**. Decoding the question helps to ensure that your answer is relevant and refers to what you have been asked.

TOP TIP UNDERSTAND EXAM LANGUAGE

Get used to exam and essay-style language by looking at specimen questions and the words they use. For example:

Exam speak	Means?	Example
'convey ideas'	*'get across a point to the reader'*: usually you have to say how this is done	Miller conveys the idea of a society at war with itself in the violent language used by the villagers towards one another, and in his own notes about the historical background.
'methods, techniques, ways'	The *'things'* the writer does: for example, a powerful description, introducing a shocking event, how someone speaks	The imaginative use of stage directions, as when Miller describes Proctor and Elizabeth in a 'spinning world ... beyond sorrow, above it' (Act Four), is a further way of conveying their emotional closeness.
'present, represent'	*'present'*: *'the way things are told to us'* *'represent'*: *'what those things might mean underneath'*	Miller presents Hale's arrival in Act One, 'loaded down with half a dozen heavy books'. The books represent not just religious authority, but also the educated, outside world from which Hale has come. However, their weight might also represent a burden that the community will have to carry.

TOP TIP 'BREAK DOWN' THE QUESTION

Pick out the **key words** or phrases. For example:

Question: How does Miller **explore** the theme of personal **envy and resentment** within the **community of Salem**?

● **Explore** – how does Miller develop this theme through characters and actions?
● **Envy and resentment** – these are the specific themes (being angered that others have more than you, and wanting what they have for yourself)
● **Community of Salem** – within the village/town

What does this tell you?

● **Focus on:** Putnam's quarrels over land; Ann Putnam's bitterness towards Rebecca and her family; Abigail's desire for John Proctor, who has rejected her, and her resentment of Elizabeth; perhaps also Elizabeth's initial resentment of what has happened in the past.

TOP TIP KNOW YOUR LITERARY LANGUAGE!

When studying texts you will come across words such as **theme, symbol, imagery, metaphor**. Some of these words could come up in the question you are asked. Make sure you know what they mean before you use them!

Planning your answer

It is vital that you **plan** your response to possible exam questions or controlled assessment tasks carefully, and then follow your plan, if you are to gain higher grades.

TOP TIP DO THE RESEARCH!

When revising for the exam or planning your response to the controlled assessment task, collect **evidence** (for example, quotations) that will support what you have to say. For example, if preparing to answer a question on the theme of conflict within the community you might list ideas as follows:

Key point	Evidence/quotation	Page/chapter, etc.
The conflict between decent working people and the authority of the law	*Judge Hathorne enters. He is in his sixties, a bitter, remorseless Salem judge.* Hathorne: 'How do you dare come roarin' into this court! Are you gone daft, Corey!'	Act Three/page 68

TOP TIP PLAN FOR PARAGRAPHS

Use paragraphs to plan your answer. For example:

❶ The first paragraph should **introduce** the **argument** you wish to make.

❷ Then, **develop** this argument with further paragraphs. Include **details**, **examples** and other possible **points of view**, making one point per paragraph.

❸ **Sum up** your argument in the last paragraph.

For example, for the following task:

Question: Discuss the significance of the relationship between Abigail and Proctor.

- Paragraph 1: *Introduction*, e.g. explain who Abigail and Proctor are, and what we know of their previous affair.

- Paragraph 2: *First point*, e.g. physical desire between them, and how that has created conflict between Proctor and his wife.

- Paragraph 3: *Second point*, e.g. how Proctor's rejection of Abigail drives her to even greater lies and deception.

- Paragraph 4: *Third point*, e.g. how their paths separate as Proctor tries to redeem his relationship with Elizabeth and Abigail focuses her power on self-preservation.

- Paragraph 5: *Fourth point*, e.g. how their individual stories end – Proctor and Elizabeth reconciled, but Proctor hanged; Abigail reported to have run off with her uncle's money.

- Paragraph 6: *Conclusion*, e.g. sum up how their relationship reflects key themes of envy, conflict and power struggles within the village.

How to use quotations

One of the secrets of success in writing essays is to use quotations **effectively**. There are five basic principles:

❶ Put quotation marks, i.e. ' ', around the quotation.

❷ Write the quotation exactly as it appears in the original.

❸ Do not use a quotation that repeats what you have just written.

❹ Use the quotation so that it fits into your sentence, or if it is longer, indent it as a separate paragraph.

❺ Only quote what is most useful.

TOP TIP **USE QUOTATIONS TO DEVELOP YOUR ARGUMENT**

Quotations should be used to develop the line of thought in your essays. Your comment should not duplicate what is in your quotation. For example:

GRADE D/E

(simply repeats the idea)
Proctor says he would rather injure himself than have a relationship with Abigail again: 'I will cut off my hand before I'll ever reach for you again.'

GRADE C

(makes a point and supports it with a relevant quotation)
Proctor rejects Abigail once and for all, using a violent image to make the point. He tells her, 'I will cut off my hand before I'll ever reach for you again.'

However, the most sophisticated way of using the writer's words is to embed them into your sentence, and further develop the point:

GRADE A

(makes point, embeds quote and develops idea)
Proctor rejects Abigail once and for all, using a violent image to make the point, telling her that he would 'cut off [his] hand' before he'd 'ever reach for [her] again'. This image, suggesting punishment and physical harm, is also symbolic of the terrible outcome of their conflict.

When you use quotations in this way, you are demonstrating the ability to use text as evidence to support your ideas – not simply including words from the original to prove you have read it.

EXAMINER'S TIP

Try to use a quotation to begin your response to a question. You can use it as a springboard for your own ideas, or as an idea you are going to argue against.

Sitting the examination

Examination papers are carefully designed to give you the opportunity to do your best. Follow these handy hints for exam success:

 BEFORE YOU START

- Make sure that you **know the texts** you are writing about so that you are properly prepared and equipped.

- You need to be **comfortable** and **free from distractions**. Inform the invigilator if anything is off-putting, e.g. a shaky desk.

- **Read** and follow the instructions, or rubric, on the front of the examination paper. You should know by now what you need to do but **check** to reassure yourself.

- Before beginning your answer have a **skim** through the **whole paper** to make sure you don't miss anything **important**.

- Observe the **time allocation** – and follow it carefully. If the paper recommends 45 minutes for a particular question on a text make sure this is how long you spend.

 WRITING YOUR RESPONSES

A typical 45 minutes examination essay is between 500 and 750 words long.

Ideally, spend a minimum 3–4 minutes planning your answer before you begin.

Use the questions to structure your response. Here is an example:

Question: What does Miller tell us about the society/setting of Salem which allows the girls' stories to be believed?

- The introduction to your answer could briefly describe where Salem was, and the **historical background**; for example, how people had fled England to set up their own perfect religious communities, and how this went wrong;

- the second part could explain the type of society and how **oppressive** it is, and how vanity and pride play a significant part;

- the third part could be an exploration of the **negative** aspects;

- the conclusion would **sum up your own viewpoint**.

For each part allocate paragraphs to cover the points you wish to make (see **Planning your answer**).

Keep your writing clear and easy to read, using paragraphs and link words to show the structure of your answer.

Spend a couple of minutes afterwards quickly checking for obvious errors.

 **'KEY WORDS' ARE THE KEY!**

Keep mentioning the **key words** from the question in your answer. This will keep you on track and remind the examiner that you are answering the question set.

> **EXAMINER'S TIP**
>
> You should focus on the question that has been set. It's crucial that you provide an answer that addresses the specific question rather than a general one including everything you know about the play!

Sitting the controlled assessment

It may be the case that you are responding to *The Crucible* in a controlled assessment situation. Follow these useful tips for success.

 KNOW WHAT YOU ARE REQUIRED TO DO

- Make sure you are clear about:
- The **specific text** and **task** you are preparing (is it on just *The Crucible*, or more than one text?)
- How **long** you have during the assessment period (i.e. 3–4 hours?)
- How **much** you are expected or allowed to write (i.e. 1,200 words?)
- **What** you are **allowed to take** into the controlled assessment, and what you can use (or not, as the case may be!). You may be able to take in brief notes **but not** draft answers, so check with your teacher.

KNOW HOW YOU CAN PREPARE

Once you know your task, topic and text/s you can:

- Make **notes** and **prepare** the **points**, **evidence**, **quotations**, etc. you are likely to use.
- Practise or draft **model answers**.
- Use these **York Notes** to hone your **skills**, e.g. use of quotations, how to plan an answer and focus on what makes a **top grade**.

DURING THE CONTROLLED ASSESSMENT

Remember:

- **Stick** to the **topic** and task you have been given.
- The allocated **time** is for **writing**, so make the most of it. It is double the time you might have in an exam, so you will be writing almost **twice as much** (or more).
- At the end of the controlled assessment follow your **teacher's instructions**. For example, make sure you have written your **name** clearly on all the pages you hand in.

GRADE BOOSTER

Where appropriate, refer to the language technique used by the writer and the effect it creates. It is just as important to say what effect a metaphor has as to be able to spot one.

Improve your grade

It is useful to know the type of responses examiners are looking for when they award different grades. The following broad guidance should help you to improve your grade when responding to the questions you are set!

GRADE C

What you need to show	What this means
Personal, sustained response to task and text	You include your own ideas and you write enough! You don't run out of ideas after two paragraphs.
Effective use of textual **details** to **support** your **explanations**	You generally support what you say with evidence, e.g. *When Danforth is first described, Miller presents him as someone who has authority and impact – even Giles is described as thinking, 'Danforth, who impresses him ...'* (Act Three).
Explanation of the writer's **use of language, structure, form**, etc., and the **effect on readers**	You write about the writer's use of these things. It's not enough simply to give a viewpoint. So, you might comment on how **religious language or references** are used in everyday speech. For example, Elizabeth says of Abigail, 'where she walks the crowd will part like the sea for Israel ...' (Act Two).
Appropriate comment on characters, plot, themes, and settings	What you say is relevant and is easy for the examiner to follow. If the task asks you to comment on how Reverend Hale is presented, that is who you write about.

GRADE A

What you need to show *in addition* to the above	What this means
Ability to **show insights into** the text and **explore alternative** responses	You look beyond the obvious. You might question whether Abigail is a scheming young woman who enjoys her power over the community, or is in fact a victim herself – having seen her own parents killed, and having been used and rejected by Proctor.
Close analysis and apt selection of **textual detail**	If you are looking at Miller's use of language, you carefully select and comment on each word in a line or phrase drawing out its distinctive effect on the reader, e.g. *When Abigail says that John 'sweated like a stallion' whenever she came near him, the rural image is especially effective in showing people controlled by animal desires and passions* (Act One).
Confident and **imaginative interpretation**	Your viewpoint is likely to convince the examiner. You show you have engaged with the text, and come up with your own ideas. These may be based on what you have discussed in class or read about, but you have made your own decisions.

Annotated sample answers

This section provides you with extracts from two **model answers**, one at **C grade** and one at **A grade**, to give you an idea of what is required to **achieve** different levels.

Question: To what extent is Abigail responsible for the terrible events in Salem?

CANDIDATE 1

Abigail is involved in lots of the things that happen in the play so in a way we can say that she is responsible. But I will look at these events one by one to see if she is really to blame.

Introduces character but point is a little vague

For a start, Abigail appears at the beginning of Act One when Parris is trying to wake his daughter Betty. Abigail admits that she, Betty and others 'did dance' in the forest but denies it was witchcraft. This is important because later when she thinks she is going to hang she changes her story. But now she just says, 'we never conjured spirits.'

Good link to later events but no conclusion drawn

It is clear that she has a lot of power over the other girls. She threatens them with violence and they believe her because she saw her own parents killed by Indians. She does this because she doesn't want all the other things to come out, like that she 'drank a charm to kill John Proctor's wife'. So from the start she is trying to protect herself.

Important point backed up by evidence

Quote embedded in point

When she meets John Proctor, who she has had an affair with, she obviously still wants him to be her lover but Arthur Miller says she has a 'wicked air.' This makes it seem like she knows what she is doing and is stirring up trouble, but perhaps she just loves John? To be fair to her she does also say that Elizabeth, Proctor's wife, is saying bad things about her. 'She is blackening my name in the village!' she says.

More needs to be made of this point

Good quote but rather clumsily expressed

However, although this may be true the key moment comes when Abigail decides that the only way to save herself is to confess that she 'danced for the Devil.' She then names lots of women to get attention away from her. This is the real start of the accusations.

Effective change to new point

Good point but needs to be developed

Later her powerful performance when Danforth questions her in Act Three and she pretends to see a 'yellow bird' which is Mary as a spirit attacking her shows she is really cunning. This is also very significant because she destroys Mary's will.

New point

At the end of the play we find out she has stolen her uncle's money and run off. But by then the damage is done and she has caused lots of the bad things to happen, including Proctor's imprisonment which leads to death. So she is responsible in many ways.

Important point but why mention it?

Answers essay title but a bit of a sudden ending!

Overall comment: This is a reasonably well-structured response which describes some of the events Abigail influences in the play. However, although the student mentions how Abigail herself might be a victim, this is not really explored sufficiently. Also, some more reference to how she is presented by Miller in the language he uses would help. There are some good points supported by some useful quotations, however, and with a better, more fluent beginning and ending, this could gain much higher marks.

GRADE C

CANDIDATE 2

Excellent opening statement which sets up the essay

Apt quotation embedded into the sentence

Well-chosen quote but what about her beauty?

Focuses on key moment at the start

Good literary term used appropriately, but is it her or the girls as a whole who are symbols?

Apt quote to support point

Abigail is clearly the catalyst for many of the awful events that occur in the play. While she can be seen as to some extent the victim of circumstances, she does enough harm on her own to be considered guilty.

Firstly, while it is true that the dancing in the forest was probably just over-excitable girls looking for an escape, she had her own reasons for being there, and 'drank a charm to kill John Proctor's wife!' as Betty claims in Act One. So, it would be fair to say that she has a 'motive' for what she does! In fact, if we look at the way Miller describes her, he seems keen to present her bad intentions – the stage directions saying she has an 'endless capacity for dissembling', which the audience sees as the play goes on. Later, when she meets with John, the writer says she has a 'wicked air' and she seems to be trying to seduce John with her charms.

Her behaviour once she is put in the spotlight by Parris and Hale over the dancing in the forest is what really gets things going, though. Once she realises she herself is under threat, she is quick to name Sarah Good, Goody Osburn and Bridget Bishop and confess that she 'danced with the Devil' at the same time as hypocritically welcoming God into her life!

Nevertheless, perhaps she had no choice. Parris has already wondered why 'no other family' has wanted her as a maid, and has heard rumours about her character. As an orphan, she may feel that she has no one she can turn to – except John – and then he rejects her.

But does this excuse her taking things so far? The way she threatens and intimidates the other girls saying she'll come to them in the 'black of some terrible night' (Act One) if they don't do as she says, shows her power. Later when they all follow her lead as she sees the 'yellow bird' in Act Three, she seems to symbolise the idea of hysteria. Without the girls' group response when they all feign being attacked by Mary, would Danforth have believed in the Devil?

After Act Three we do not see her again. We find out from Parris that she has run off, after robbing him of thirty pounds and he is left 'penniless'. Why she has done this is not made clear, but perhaps she believed her luck could not last. And the audience might remember back to the first scene when Miller describes her 'ill-concealed resentment' for her uncle. It is resentment for Proctor, for Elizabeth, for the whole village that makes her as responsible as anyone for what happens.

Answers one of the bullets in the task

Good alternative point of view, but could be developed

Excellent link to start

Answers task question in last line

Overall comment: This is a really excellent response. Abigail's part in the play is explained clearly, as are her possible motives for behaving as she does. The close reference to Miller's stage directions helps to paint a picture of her, although a little more could be made of her symbolic role in the play. The candidate forgets to mention that she is 'strikingly beautiful' too, a key element in the relationship between Proctor and his wife. It might also be worth exploring who else could be considered responsible for the events, even if only in passing – Hale's and Parris's weakness, Putnam's envy, and Danforth's defending of his position could have been briefly mentioned and this is perhaps what prevents the highest mark possible.

GRADE A

Further questions

EXAM-STYLE QUESTIONS

The following exam-style questions are based on the format used by exam boards.

❶ Abigail Williams is described by Proctor as being 'a lump of vanity' (p. 89). How does Miller present Abigail? Is she vain from your point of view?

❷ To what extent is Elizabeth's appearance in Act Three to support John in court a turning point in the play?

❸ In what different ways does Miller present a community that is in conflict in the play?

❹ 'Reverend Hale is a weak, foolish man who causes the tragic events of the play.' To what extent is this an accurate description of how Hale is presented?

❺ Discuss the effectiveness of Miller's use of language and voice in creating a sense of a particular society.

❻ How important are the themes of envy and greed in the play as a whole?

❼ To what extent does religious language – words, phrases, constructions, etc. – play an important role in the way ideas are expressed?

❽ How does Miller present the changing relationship of Proctor and Elizabeth over the course of the play?

CONTROLLED ASSESSMENT-STYLE TASKS

Below are two sample controlled assessment tasks. It is likely that you will be sitting an exam on *The Crucible* rather than doing a controlled assessment, but you may still find it useful to practise these tasks as part of your revision.

❶ Characterisation and voice. Explore the way a central character is presented in a text you have studied, for example:

How is Proctor presented in the film version of *The Crucible*? How does Daniel Day-Lewis interpret the role? What aspects of Proctor's character does he bring out?

❷ Themes and ideas. Discuss the theme of power and authority in a text you have studied. For example:

How do Danforth and Abigail in their different ways demonstrate their power over others?

Literary terms

Literary term	Explanation
allegory	a story that can be seen to have two different and parallel meanings, rather like a fable or parable. *The Crucible* can be read as an allegory of the anti-Communist investigations in the United States in the 1950s
character(s)	either a person in a play, novel, etc., or his or her personality
imagery/image	a picture in words. There are two obvious kinds of image, **simile** and **metaphor**
inversion/inverted	a departure from normal word order. In *The Crucible* this is used to represent an older form of English, e.g. 'I know not what I have said', 'I like not the sound of it'
irony/ironic	using words to convey the opposite of their literal meaning, a deliberate contrast between apparent and intended meaning; also incongruity between what might be expected and what actually occurs
metaphor	a description of one thing in terms of something else, e.g. 'I have seen you looking up, burning in your loneliness' (p. 18), 'I have made a bell of my honour! I have rung the doom of my good name' (p. 89)
simile	a direct comparison of one thing with another, using 'like', 'as' or 'as if', e.g. 'The crowd will part like the sea for Israel' (p. 43)
symbol	an object, a person or a thing used to represent another thing
theme	a recurrent idea in a work of literature

Checkpoint answers

Checkpoint 1
Most of the girls were probably only playing a game, but it seems that Abigail and Tituba were dabbling in conjuring. Look for evidence of this in the play.

Checkpoint 2
Abigail has not yet seen the potential for revenge. When is the first time that we see Abigail is plotting against Elizabeth?

Checkpoint 3
She changes from girl to woman the moment he enters, taking on *a confidential, wicked air* (p. 17).

Checkpoint 4
Abigail was an orphan (her parents were killed by Indians); she had been taken in as a servant by the Proctors. John Proctor abused Abigail's and his wife's trust by taking advantage of Abigail when she was weak.

Checkpoint 5
Wily old Giles likes to be involved in whatever is going on.

Checkpoint 6
This petty quibble shows that Parris is a greedy and small-minded man.

Checkpoint 7
Common-sense Rebecca has great experience with children.

Checkpoint 8
Mrs Putnam resents Rebecca's high moral tone.

Checkpoint 9
Tituba cries out these names at the end of the Act. She is simply repeating the ideas of people in the room.

Checkpoint 10
She realises that she will be believed if she identifies witches, and she has learned about the ways witches supposedly affect their victims.

Checkpoint 11
Elizabeth is jealous of Abigail; John Proctor is embarrassed that he has been alone with her.

Checkpoint 12
Unknown to Mary, the 'poppet' is the device Abigail uses to accuse Elizabeth of witchcraft. She argues that Elizabeth made the 'poppet' as an image of her and stabbed it, causing Abigail to suffer stomach pains.

Checkpoint 13
It is clear that Abigail has accused Elizabeth.

Checkpoint 14
It reinforces Hale's doubts about the girls' testimony. Try to find evidence of Hale's doubts.

Checkpoint 15
Hale's cowardice is shown when he refuses to act upon his own suspicions. Where else is Hale seen to be weak?

Checkpoint 16
John Proctor is widely respected. Can you find evidence of this in the play?

Checkpoint 17
Hathorne is ruthless and small-minded. Identify the other characters that are portrayed negatively.

Checkpoint 18
Hathorne insists that anyone who speaks out is doing so to harm the court. This stops Hale from speaking out about the sensible nature of the complaints.

Checkpoint 19
She realises that Hale is turning the court against her.

Checkpoint 20
Abigail is so confident that she threatens the deputy-governor of the province. How does she recover from this mistake?

Checkpoint 21
She knew that she would soon be caught out and fled while there was still time.

Checkpoint 22
He has realised that it is not God's work but man's greed and envy that have prevailed in Salem.